"I am getting the distinct impression you have somewhere else you need to be."
The gold flecks in her eyes flared in the candlelight. A current of electricity ran through his veins.

"No. Please stay. I'm being a jackass. You've done nothing wrong."

Her skin turned a deep shade of pink, exposing a side of her Noah hadn't seen before. He related to it. This glimpse of vulnerability.

What if you showed her you're as vulnerable as she is?

And what if he tore off his shirt, beat his chest and admitted that he was clinging to every cell of inner alpha male he could, because if he didn't, it'd be clear for all to see that he didn't have a clue what he was doing and that he wished he had a loved one by his side who knew him inside and out? Someone who could assure him he could do this. Someone like Rebecca.

After a moment's silence she squinted at him. "I might be humiliating myself here, but do you get the feeling that your cousin is trying to set us up?"

And just like that the tension

Dear Reader,

Do you have a Happy Holiday Place? Somewhere you've been either in real life or in your mind that instantly brings a smile to your lips? Bali is (one of) mine. I was a bit of a travel nut in my twenties and it turns out I have lots of Happy Holiday Places... or maybe I just like holidays! Anyway...I wrote this during a pandemic lockdown and really wanted to capture that sense of freedom and strength that comes from the rejuvenation of a really good break from your real life. The kind that puts things in perspective. A bit like a lockdown! But one saturated in sunshine, good food and, in this case, falling in love. I thoroughly enjoyed bringing Rebecca and Noah's journey to life. Now, get out your sunglasses and factor 50... It's time to go on holiday!

xx *Annie O'*

IN BALI WITH
THE SINGLE DAD

———

ANNIE O'NEIL

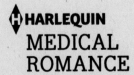

**MEDICAL
ROMANCE**

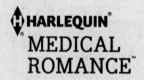

HARLEQUIN®
MEDICAL ROMANCE™

Recycling programs for this product may not exist in your area.

ISBN-13: 978-1-335-40929-4

In Bali with the Single Dad

Copyright © 2022 by Annie O'Neil

All rights reserved. No part of this book may be used or reproduced in any manner whatsoever without written permission except in the case of brief quotations embodied in critical articles and reviews.

This is a work of fiction. Names, characters, places and incidents are either the product of the author's imagination or are used fictitiously. Any resemblance to actual persons, living or dead, businesses, companies, events or locales is entirely coincidental.

For questions and comments about the quality of this book, please contact us at CustomerService@Harlequin.com.

Harlequin Enterprises ULC
22 Adelaide St. West, 41st Floor
Toronto, Ontario M5H 4E3, Canada
www.Harlequin.com

Printed in U.S.A.

Annie O'Neil spent most of her childhood with her leg draped over the family rocking chair and a book in her hand. Novels, baking and writing too much teenage angst poetry ate up most of her youth. Now Annie splits her time between corralling her husband into helping her with their cows, baking, reading, barrel racing (not really!) and spending some very happy hours at her computer, writing.

Books by Annie O'Neil

Harlequin Medical Romance

The Island Clinic
The Princess and the Pediatrician

Double Miracle at St. Nicolino's Hospital
A Family Made in Rome

Dolphin Cove Vets
The Vet's Secret Son

Miracles in the Making
Risking Her Heart on the Single Dad

Christmas Under the Northern Lights
Hawaiian Medic to Rescue His Heart
New Year Kiss with His Cinderella

Visit the Author Profile page
at Harlequin.com for more titles.

To Chantal: your friendship is a permanent ray of sunshine to me xx

CHAPTER ONE

UP UNTIL NOW, life had never given Rebecca Stone cause to believe in lust at first sight, let alone love at first sight. Sensible was as sensible did, in her book. But today she was a believer. In the lust part anyway.

Flickers of heat were dancing about her erogenous zones as if she were a teenage girl about to be kissed by the lead singer of a boy band. Extraordinary, considering mere seconds ago her hormones were behaving very much like the pragmatic, heartbroken, thirty-seven-year-old English doctor she was. One who was forcing herself out of her comfort zone by trying to find her Zen on a surfboard in Bali.

She looked down at her nipples. Yup. They were definitely feeling it. The sea water was simply too perfect a temperature to blame for their…erm…peaked interest. The gentle movements of the water underneath her surfboard weren't bad either. Better than the spin cycle on her washing machine, anyway. Not that she'd actually *done* that. Well… Apart from that once. Research, obviously. For science.

She looked back at the beach, hunting for the man who had triggered the initial flare of electric current.

Mmm. There he was. *Ai caramba.*

Admittedly, he wasn't exactly close, and she wasn't wearing her glasses, so there was a lot more fantasy than reality at play, but…

If gorgeous Zen gods came in six-foot-something, ebony-haired, sexily-inked, golden-skinned packages she was ready for the universe to bring them.

And the universe did. From where she sat he looked like a walking, talking action hero. Lean, fit, lethal if he wanted to be—but only because his ability to protect himself came via a martial art born of an ancient philosophy of peace that only resorted to hand-to-hand combat as a last and regretful resort.

Her secret weakness.

Not your usual go-to fantasy man for a girl born and raised in the depths of the English countryside…but everyone had their buttons, right? And hers were being pushed.

Rather than let reality deflate the fizz of lust bubbles effervescing round her insides, she lay back on her surfboard and closed her eyes, letting the ocean gently tip its warm sensations around her as if she were a lava lamp.

Ah, now… If this was what her serenity coach meant by feeling 'at one with the ocean'…*splish-splash*…she was pretty sure she was getting the hang of it. Finally.

How interesting that this newfound peaceful feeling had arrived the day before she had to decide whether to keep her ticket as it was—open-ended—or change it and head back to reality in England.

She had to pick up where she'd left off at some point. Newly single. In need of a job. At a hospital, probably. It would be different enough from what she was meant to be doing to take away some of the sting.

It wasn't as if the world and the life she'd left behind had entirely evaporated simply because she was thousands of miles away.

No. It would still be there. But it wouldn't be the same.

Her thumb shifted to her ring finger and felt the absence of the ring anew.

A skittering of unwelcome goosebumps surfaced as she tried to picture herself getting off the plane in England.

Could she even rely on her gut instinct any more? The one that had led her to paediatric surgery but then taken a hard right into general practice.

The core-deep instinct she'd relied on when she'd worked with her young patients had definitely been broken when she picked her fiancé. She'd been so *sensible* about their relationship. So *practical.*

Maybe that had been the problem.

She tried to imagine their last moments together with a new fictional twist. One in which she swept the ring off her finger and coolly placed it on the counter. Throwing it was a step too far into melodrama for her sensibilities. *Have your ring*, she'd say in this version, continuing in a calm, powerful, yet astonishingly sultry movie-star-style voice. *May it serve as a bittersweet reminder of everything you've left behind.*

She grinned and gave the air a little victory punch, letting her fingers splash back into the sea with a satisfying *splosh.* Yes, that version of herself was rather delightful. One worth pursuing. Definitely better than the version who'd been blotchy-faced and tear-streaked as she'd soaped her finger so she could yank the ring off her finger, repeating over and over, 'You found someone else? Wasn't I enough?' She'd happily leave that girl behind.

If only this new version of herself could

empty her brain of practical thoughts and be more whimsical and carefree, like her new surf buddy Kylie. Kylie wouldn't be thinking about the tide being about to shift, and the fact that falling asleep on top of a surfboard not only increased her chances of sunburn but meant she might literally be swept out into the vast expanse that was the Indian Ocean, never to be found again.

And just like that here calamity brain kicked into gear. What if she got so Zenned out the waves crashed over her and she drowned? What would become of her beloved Nanny Bea? The patients she was meant to help? The soulmate she was—*please, God*—destined to meet? The children she was meant to have even though the clock was ticking insanely fast on that front and realistically, as a doctor, she knew her chances were dwindling—

Stop!

None of that was happening. Not here. Not now.

She forced herself to take slow, deep breaths with her eyes closed. Maybe if she counted down from ten in time with the swish-swish of the sea. Ten…nine…eight…lucky seven…

Perhaps Mr Tall, Dark and Dangerously Sexy would come out and save her. She cracked her eyes open again and, as if he'd been a mirage, there was no sign of him. Hope plummeted heavily into her belly. No chance of a rescue, then.

At least the cove was every bit as beautiful.

There were a bounty of idyllic tropical coves here in Bali, but this one was particularly divine. Steep rock cliffs covered in lush jungle greenery cocooned an immaculate white beach. It was perfect for swimmers of all levels, and had some ace waves if you swam out further, and it had the added bonus of being only a short walk from the all-female surfing school and resort where she was staying.

'Bex!'

Rebecca pushed herself up and waved at Kylie. She still wasn't used to being called by the nickname. Any nickname, really. She'd never had one. Had always been plain old Rebecca Stone.

That's Dr *Rebecca Stone, young lady,* she heard her Nan counter. *No one can take that away from you.*

'Earth to The Bexinator?' Kylie spoke in a robotic voice. 'The ocean is calling me. Is it calling you?'

'Seriously?' Rebecca frowned out at the surf, then at Kylie. They'd surfed all morning, eaten like wolves, sweated through so-called Recovery Yoga, and then, at Kylie's request, come out to the cove for another hour of intense surfing.

With the tide receding, swimming out to the rideable waves would be a longer, more dangerous paddle—hello, riptides! As much as twenty-something Kylie seemed like the Energizer Bunny, everyone had their limits. Especially newer surfers. Like Rebecca.

'Are you sure you're not too tired?' Rebecca swung her hands in invitation. 'Come here. Bob alongside me and soak in the sights. Maybe we can spot some new eye candy.'

She tipped her head towards the cove, where… *Ooh!* Her eyes caught and snagged on her sexy mystery man. Only this time he had company. Two little ebony-haired girls were balancing on his feet and clutching his hands as he floated them through gales of laughter onto the beach. She sighed. He looked like a living statue made of precious metals. If she wasn't completely rusty in the flirtation department, she'd—

A blonde woman with alabaster skin peeking out from a sarong entered the cove and ran towards him with a couple of beach towels.

Rebecca's breath caught in her throat like shards of glass. Whether or not she could flirt didn't matter. He wasn't available. If only she'd known that about her fiancé.

Oblivious, Kylie clucked. 'No eye candy for me. Remember? I'm all loved-up.'

'Hmmm…' Rebecca feigned ignorance. 'Remind me?'

Kylie play-punched her arm.

Rebecca laughed good-naturedly and they air-boxed for a minute.

There wasn't a soul on Bali who wasn't aware that Kylie was loved-up. Except maybe the guy on the beach. From her vantage point there wasn't a thing in the world he needed, let alone tourist love gossip. Or, in her case, a lack thereof.

Her eyes drifted from him to the little girls. To their glossy black hair, swinging along their backs. The way they were practically glued to his side, looking up at him, laughing, dangling off his muscled forearms like pretty giggling ornaments. She ached to know what that felt like. That deep, biological love that only came from being a family—

You've got your gran. Some people don't even have that.

She tore her eyes away before unwelcome tears began to trickle down her cheeks. You'd think by now she'd be immune to seeing men with children without her ovaries waving and doing silly dances, screaming, *Me, too! Me, too! I want to go to that party!* But, no. It appeared her ovaries were still very much wanting to join the party, despite their decreasing ability to make babies of her own.

Thanks, life.

She caught the dark thought and forced it into a new form—just as the resort's serenity coach had recommended. *'Take unwelcome thoughts and turn them into mind clay. Reshape them into something different. Something positive.'*

Wrapping the blob of dark thoughts in a swatch of happy thoughts was simple enough on a practical level. She was two weeks into her holiday on Bali. One she could easily extend as there was literally nothing waiting for her at home—apart from her nan, who had offered to come out to Bali if she wanted to stay longer. She had always been a sensible saver, never over-extending her finances—not even on her wedding dress, returned now, courtesy of the wedding insurance she'd purchased. The wedding fund she'd begun the day she'd turned eighteen had now been renamed The No More Comfort Zone Fund, and still had a fair amount of savings in it.

It was an enviable place to be. She had the whole of the rest of her life ahead of her. Minus the thirty-seven years she'd already had. But if she lived to a hundred, thirty-seven wasn't even half her life.

Hmmm… The dark thoughts were still peeking out.

She scraped around for one more thing to cover up the darkness.

Her hair! Her hair was like a different creature here. Maybe it was something in the water. Maybe it was the fact that she'd forgotten her straighteners and blow dryer and was wearing it wild and free, like a costume drama heroine. Whatever it was, her hair had transformed itself from the bane of her existence into a huge wavy halo of fire-coloured locks.

So! She had her health, a savings account, and she was bossing it on the hair front. Just because David, his solitaire diamond ring and the entire, very specific future they'd planned together weren't on the cards any more, it didn't mean her future couldn't be rose-coloured.

Sure. The break-up might have changed her from a proactive, list-making, uber-achiever into something cracked and fragile. But, courtesy of an intervention from her grandmother in the form of a plane ticket to the most exotic place she could think of, the drowning her sorrows phase was over.

'It's a life gift,' her grandmother had said. *'And life,'* she had reminded her granddaughter with a tap on the nose, *'is for living.'*

So here she was, slowly rebuilding herself, relighting her internal fires, and in the process trying to learn how to become more flexible and resilient. She'd learnt the hard way that keeping her eyes on one solitary prize had blinkered her to the things she should have noticed. Like the fact her ex didn't love her any more and had been having a year-long affair with someone he *did* love.

Anyway...

Her eyes slipped back to the shore. There were other prizes out there. Better, more appropriate prizes. Not that a husband was a prize. Or a gift. Or something that finally made you whole. A husband—any partner, really—should be a soulmate. A kindred spirit. A best friend. And David hadn't been any of those things in the end. A good actor was what he'd been.

None of which meant she couldn't enjoy a little bit of eye candy from a distance, right?

Straight away she found him again. The sexy dad.

A hot, biological jolt of connection sparked through her when he turned to face the sea and—against the odds—appeared to be looking directly at her. He was still too far away for her to properly read his expression, but...and she didn't know why...the funniest feeling came over her. One of empathy. A sense that Mr Perfect hadn't always been that way.

Perhaps he, too, had been someone entirely different before he'd arrived here on this beach with his two beautiful daughters and his gorgeous blonde wife. A monk? A soldier fighting for his life? A clueless fiancé who had thought his life was perfect only to find out everything he'd been working towards had been an illusion?

She pulled a face. She was definitely going to have to work on her positive visualisation.

Rebecca summoned up a smile and retrained her gaze on Kylie, who was checking her board leash was secure. 'Kylie…? I'm knackered. You've surfed as much as me today. Are you sure you're up for another run?'

Kylie gave a huge affirmative nod. 'I told the Surf God I wasn't going to meet him until I've done it properly.'

'Because you want to prove to *yourself* you can do it, right?'

Rebecca was all for a holiday romance, but not the kind that meant you'd do something stupid. The Surf God—aka Antonio, an Italian beach bum—was the most recent of Kylie's *innamoratos*. Something about him seemed a bit too slippery eel for Rebecca. Or maybe she was just jaded.

Kylie rolled her eyes and scoffed. 'Totes. Who else would I do this for?' She gave Rebecca a cautionary look. Kylie knew her history courtesy of one too many margaritas the other night. 'Surf gods come and go, Bex. But I'm the one who lives in my skin, so this is for me and those juicy little waves out there. The ones with my name written all over them.'

Rebecca grinned and met Kylie's fist-bump. Whatever happened, the one thing Rebecca was certain of was that Kylie was a gift from the universe.

When she'd first arrived at the resort, all sad and heartbroken, Kylie had been sitting out on the shared deck and had invited her over for sundowners. Over brightly coloured cocktails she'd waxed lyrical about meeting her 'for ever man' on her very first night out in Kuta, the island's biggest resort town. A bartender who made a mean Sex on the Beach. Stefan? Sven? Didn't matter. He'd taken up with someone else, and so had Kylie.

Who knew who next week might bring? Conor the chiropractor? Declan the dentist? Both? Whomsoever she chose, Kylie always made one thing very, very clear. Kylie was in charge of Kylie's heart. No one else. It was a lesson Rebecca had vowed to put into practice if and when she ever fell in love again. If that was what she'd even shared with David. Had it been love? Her nipples had never pinged to attention when David was within kissing distance.

Kylie shadowed her eyes against the afternoon sun. 'You're not going to your dark place, are you?'

Rebecca wasn't sure where she was. But it definitely wasn't dark.

When she didn't answer, Kylie flicked her thumb out towards the setting sun. 'Sure you don't want a final ride?'

Rebecca raised her arms then let them flop back to her sides, 'Honestly. I'm good. My arms have had their fill of fighting the waves today.'

'Noodled, are you?'

Rebecca grinned. She had doubled her surf slang since she'd arrived, and this was one of her favourite words: noodled. 'Tired arms, but I'm a happy little camper. Go on. The sooner you catch that wave, the sooner we can have sundowners back at the resort.'

Non-alcoholic sundowners. She'd had enough of chasing the blues away with vodka.

She gave Kylie a jaunty farewell salute and watched as her holiday friend paddled off.

Kylie was not only ten years younger than her, she was positively alight with oxytocin—the so-called 'love hormone'. A definite advantage. Not Rebecca. No oxytocin in her. Not so much as a droplet. Oxytocin was dead to her.

And just like that she was hunting for Hot Dad and his little girls again.

Ping!

There they were. Building a sandcastle.

She closed her eyes as a twist of something too close to envy tightened in her belly. Jagged shards of broken dreams crashed through her like pieces of icy dislodged metal. Harsh and bruising. Destabilising.

She let out a small growl and shook the sensation away. She had the sun on her shoulders, a tropical sea lapping round her legs and a hotel room on stilts waiting for her. And cocktail hour with a top-rate gal-pal who had never once blown off their sundowner sessions for a guy. From here on out she'd take her cues from Kylie. She would be spontaneous, carefree, and pay attention to the gifts the universe was offering.

Sure, Sexy Dad was unavailable. But perhaps she was meant simply to enjoy the aesthetic pleasure of him. It wasn't like he was the type of man she went for in 'real' life.

The thought snagged in her mind and made her double back.

Her serenity coach had repeatedly told Rebecca she was too closed off to things she wasn't familiar with. Change-resistant.

A smile twitched at her lips. Well, then… Sexy Dad's mission was complete. She officially knew what it was like to have her body gripped by lust at first sight.

Her smile stretched into a self-effacing grimace as she remembered the childish tantrum she'd had in front of her nan. *'Never Again! No more men! Not even if the man of my dreams walks through that door! I am done!'*

Well… At the time she'd meant it.

Who was she to fight it if the universe was offering her a man wearing board shorts as if they'd been specially tailored for him? One who had a six-pack and enigmatic script inked round his to-die-for biceps? Not to mention the ebony clutch of man bun resting at the top of his head. She'd always been a 'short haircuts for guys' kind of woman, but this guy? He was the exception to the unwritten rule.

See? *Ha!* Step by step…wave by wave…gorgeous unavailable sex god by sex god…the nightmare that had been her life back in England was being churned out of her system. One scrumptious man bun at a time.

She nodded in the direction she thought the UK was and lifted her hands in a prayer of thanks to her grandmother.

If it hadn't been for Nanny Bea she would've been climbing up Machu Picchu about now. Getting blisters and altitude sickness, most likely. Sleeping in a tent instead of a teak four-poster bed with mosquito netting wafting gently in the breeze. Or, more likely, not sleeping, and wondering why on earth she'd tortured herself by going on her honeymoon on her own. So the switch to Bali had been a good thing. Far better than wallowing in misery under her duvet after her fiancé had got someone else pregnant and moved to London so they could live out their lives in wedded bliss.

She closed her eyes, instantly hearing her grandmother's strong country brogue countering the dark thoughts pressing for head space.

'Life's what you make of it, Rebecca. If you want a prize for sitting out the next fifty-odd years in that tatty old armchair so be it, but I won't be the one handing out ribbons.'

The admonishment had been enough to make her take a shower. Which had been a win at that juncture. The next day she'd combed her hair. The next she'd actually gone to the shops. Sure, it had only been to buy ingredients to make brownies, which she'd eaten straight from the pan, but even so… She was learning to count her blessings where she found them these days. Not counting her chickens before they hatched.

She looked back to the shore.

Beach Towel Woman had disappeared, and it was just Hot Dad and his little girls now. His back was to her—exquisite musculature, undulating beneath skin that was a warm copper hue and then inch by inch disappearing beneath a long-sleeved shirt. *Sigh.*

After they'd taken turns painting one another's faces with sunblock, he stretched out and propped himself up on his elbows, whereupon the girls delighted in making his long, distinctly muscular, and very attractive legs and torso disappear under handful after handful of white sand.

Not that she was letting her gaze linger, or anything, but she couldn't help but notice the way he held his shoulders. The proud lift of his spine. There was a tautness to it that spoke of… She shook her head, unable to put her finger on it. Discipline? Penance? Whatever it was, that peculiar sense of familiarity took flight again and rippled through her central nervous system.

Another wave caught the edge of her board, reminding her that bobbing about in the thick of things probably wasn't the best of ideas when other surfers might be whizzing in off some of the bigger waves.

She pressed her palms onto the board, and was just about to start paddling to shore when she saw Kylie coming in on a wave, her face beaming with joy at having finally managed to stand up.

Another surfer, a young man wearing flower print board shorts, joined the wave from the other side. Uh-oh. Rookie error. This wasn't good. She could tell Kylie thought she was on the wave alone, and the other guy, from the way he was manipulating his board to ride the wave all the way to shore, thought he had the advantage. They didn't call that kind of move snaking for no reason.

She tried to call out to Kylie, but the crashing of the surf drowned out her warning. She was too late to stop the inevitable. The front of the guy's board clipped the back of Kylie's. Both boards flipped up, obscuring her view of the surfers.

Rebecca flattened herself to her board and began to paddle with everything she had.

CHAPTER TWO

NOAH WHIPPED ROUND, his sand 'blanket' sliding down his legs, to the obvious disappointment of his nieces. But the sharp chorus of groans and cries of alarm that had just swept across the cove had him on high alert.

'Uncle Noah!' Isla cried. 'Where are you going?'

Ruby grabbed his hand. 'You're not going to leave us, are you?'

Noah froze, the small little-girl hands in his making more of an impression than he could have ever predicted.

The man he'd been two months ago would've been halfway down the beach by now. Ready to launch himself into the sea and plough through the waves to help. He'd operated on enough surfers to know how bad some of their injuries could be.

But he couldn't be that guy any more. Mr

Drop Everything and Run. Or, more accurately, Mr Drop Every*one* and Run.

He had responsibilities now. Beyond anything he'd ever shouldered. Dependents. Little girls with his sister's big black eyes looking up at him, their anxiety cutting through the fun they'd just been sharing. Feeling the fear that, yet again, someone they loved would never come back.

'No. I'm staying here with you two, but…'

Their eyes widened, then creased with fear. Any sentence that had a 'but' wasn't making a turn for the better.

'But we might have to head to the clinic, okay? Together.'

'What about the picnic?'

'We can still eat it,' Noah assured them. 'Just…maybe in the Jeep.'

His suggestion was met with forlorn little 'ohs'.

He scrambled to think of something they'd like even while steering them back onto his feet, so he could edge his way closer to the shore in case he was needed. 'What if we have it by the pool back at the villa? Or try again tomorrow?'

'I suppose…' sighed Isla.

'Okay,' Ruby managed, through a chin-quiver.

He pulled her in close and dropped an awkward kiss on her head. It was what his sister would've done, right?

Not for the first time he cursed himself for delaying, and then skipping, her multiple invitations to come to the island for family time with them. It wasn't as if he was a stranger to the place. He'd used to come every year when his mum was—

Anyway… Too late, he finally saw that all of the time he'd spent in the operating theatre back in Sydney, instead of here getting to know his sister's children, would have been worth its weight in gold.

Big fat tears began to streak down six-year-old Ruby's cheeks.

Crumbs. He pulled them both in close but said nothing. He owed these two some fun time. He'd relied on his brother-in-law's relatives and his cousin too much over the past couple of months. *He* was meant to be their guardian now. Their de facto father. And he'd promised them an afternoon at the beach.

Failed at the first hurdle. Nice one.

More shouts erupted from the shore.

'We'll come back tomorrow,' he assured them, as he tried to figure out who was in trouble and where. 'And tonight we can have…um…. ice cream? Ice cream sundaes.' He knew he sounded distracted. Was plucking things from the *Parenting from Hell* rulebook, but…

'They're both down!'

'I see blood.'

'Aren't there sharks round here?'

'Someone should call an ambulance!'

'Are there any doctors here?'

What the hell was he supposed to do?

Did he stay there, safe on the beach with the girls, or follow his oath as a doctor to prioritise the patient?

He didn't have a patient yet. And he'd also pledged to maintain the utmost respect for human life. Didn't that include Ruby and Isla? He didn't know any more. The lines between his professional and personal lives had more than blurred over the past ten years. They'd pretty much disappeared. His professional life had *been* his personal life right up until he'd got that phone call.

He felt as if he was being ripped in half. How the hell did parents do anything beyond prioritising their kids?

He forced his brain to stop whirling. He was a sought-after surgeon, for heaven's sake. He knew how to prioritise.

Right. Number one: he wasn't the only able-bodied swimmer in the small cove. There were multiple people out on the water already. And now that his cousin Mel had gone back to the clinic there was no one here he knew—let alone trusted to look after the girls. Which meant the only person they had to protect them was him.

Much to his horror, his first instinct hadn't been to stay glued to their sides. Already he was failing them. Failing his sister's memory.

Today was meant to have been just for them. His first full day off since he'd arrived in Bali—excluding the funeral, of course. A huge, elaborate multi-day affair, complete with a ceremonial burial, a procession and a funeral pyre, then a ceremony by the sea where the waves had escorted his sister and his brother-in-law's souls to a higher plane.

Half the island's population had come out to pay their respects. Except, of course, the driver of the four-by-four that had sent their car over the edge of the narrow mountain road and tumbling down a ravine. He was in prison now. Serving a life sentence during which the erstwhile tourist could reflect on just how wise his decision to get stoned and barrel down a road full of switchbacks 'just to see what the rental car could handle' had been.

Noah's first instinct had been to close the clinic to tourists. Screw the lot of them.

Then pragmatics had kicked in. Now that he wasn't sending money from Sydney it needed an income. If the tourists' travel insurance money didn't help fund the other half of its work—the one that offered expensive surgeries to deprived local families...

He swept his hand through his hair until it jammed at the base of his bun. It went against everything he stood for to stand here and watch other people swim out to help the surfers.

'Uncle Noah?'

He looked down at Isla's sweet face. 'Yes, darlin'?'

'You can go if you want. We'll be okay. As long as you promise to come back.'

He ribcage all but caved in on itself.

'No, darlin'. I'm going to stick here with you. If they need medical help it'll be here on the beach or back at the clinic.'

Ruby's face crumpled. 'What about our bed-time stories?'

'Hey...' He dropped down onto one knee, using his thumbs to wipe the tears away. 'We'll still have story time.'

'Promise?' She held out a little finger.

'Promise.' They linked fingers and it just about destroyed him to see the relief in her eyes.

He rose and tugged his T-shirt on, silently cursing himself. This was his fault. The tears. The anxiety. Since the funeral he'd buried himself in work at the clinic, as if that would bring his sister and her husband back. Thank God his cousin had foreseen his inability to juggle both the clinic and the girls from the get-go, but now it was time to step into shoes he didn't even begin to know how to fill.

Mel had to go home to her family in Oz. His late brother-in-law's family, whilst Indonesian, lived on another island, and had left a week ago amidst a flurry of promises to come back regularly. There had been talk of sending the girls to live in Jakarta with them. Talk Noah had refused to give any sort of definitive response to. Mostly because he had no idea what was best for the girls, and that had to be his number one priority right now.

Sure. He could hire a nanny. In fact, he'd *have* to hire a nanny. Someone, anyway. He couldn't work *and* be there for them the way he wanted to. Not that work was filling the dark void inside him the way it had used to. No matter how many broken bones he set, or wounds he stitched, or coral rashes he cleaned at the clinic, nothing would bring his sister and her husband back. The same way his punishing work schedule back in Sydney hadn't cured his mother or turned his father into the kind of man who led by example. Work had come first—family second.

The past few years Noah had felt himself falling into the same trap. *Do as I say. Not as I do.*

At least he hadn't had affairs.

He screwed the memories up tight and

crammed them out of sight. What his dad did in his private time wasn't Noah's concern any more. He barely considered the man a member of his family.

The girls were his family now. This very morning he'd made a silent promise to his sister, as he and the girls had laid flowers at her shrine. A vow to ensure Ruby and Isla would know beyond a shadow of a doubt that he was there for them as much as he was for the clinic.

No.

He checked himself.

The clinic would have to—

Hell. He didn't know.

The list of things he'd do differently if he could live his life over again began to press against his temporal lobes. He'd be married with kids of his own if he hadn't been so hellbent on—on what, exactly?

Not hurting anyone the way his father had?

He looked down at the near identical pairs of ebony eyes looking up at him. Real life was here and now and shaped like two perfect little girls. Little girls who needed to know that they were loved and, just as importantly, safe.

'The guy's gonna need medical help, for sure!'

'I'm a doctor.'

He couldn't stop himself. He'd sworn an oath. He'd also signed a fifteen-page document assuring his sister that, in the unlikely event of her death, he'd become guardian to her children.

'It's all right, girls. I'm going to be right here within sight, yeah?'

'Fan-bloody-tastic, mate.' A fellow Australian jogged over to him. 'A Quimby wave hog hit the tube and blasted straight into the kook. Real sketchy. Look. There.' He pointed out to sea. 'I reckon the girl is tombstoning.'

Noah stared at him. Despite doing countless surgeries on surfers, their lingo was not his native tongue. 'Translate.'

'Idiot bloke hit a wave, thought he could out-run the newbie girl, and crashed into her instead. She's still attached to her board but must've been knocked out. Because it's surfacing and she isn't.'

Noah took a step towards the sea and felt the surfer's arm restrain him. 'No, mate. There's a couple of people already paddling out there. If you're the one who's going to stitch 'em up or blast the water out of their lungs you need to stay safe here with your little ones, yeah?'

Noah swore under his breath. Fancy getting told how to look after his nieces by a surfer dude.

The bloke continued, oblivious to the short, sharp knife-blow he'd delivered to Noah's confidence. 'I predict a smashed nose or a fin slash for him. And a concussion for her.'

Now, that was language he could understand. Orthopaedic surgeons in Australia were well acquainted with noses that had met their surfboards face-forward. He'd realigned more than one deviated septum whilst avoiding fresh sutures applied after the back fin of a surfboard had done its best to scar the surfer for life.

Why the hell people thought they could outwit the ocean was beyond him.

Running. That was more his speed. Cycling. Swimming. In a pool.

And long walks at sunset on the beach...

He could practically hear his sister dissolving into giggles as she pretended to type up imaginary profiles for him on the dating apps he'd refused to let her sign him up to after Alice had given him his walking papers.

The reminder of those moments he'd never have again made him instinctively tighten his grip on his nieces' shoulders. With one tucked under each arm, Noah squinted out to the bay, his dark eyes arrowing in on a guy flipping over his surfboard and awkwardly climbing on, face-planting on the board as a wave crashed over him. When he lifted his head, he saw his face was streaming with blood.

'Ha!' crowed the surfer dude. 'Can I call it or what?'

Noah gave him a grudging smile. It felt

strange, as lately it hadn't been in his practice to smile. Anyway... Whatever... Work. Broken nose. He could probably set it here on the beach if that was all that had happened to him. If it was anything else they'd have to head back to the clinic.

His real concern was for the woman.

He could see the other board bobbing up and down nearby, but no sign of its owner. *Not good.* Riders usually wore an ankle leash that kept them and the board together. He saw an auburn-haired woman—the one he'd caught looking at him earlier—approaching the scene on a colourful board. She was wearing a long-sleeved swimsuit.

He'd told himself that it was her suit that had caught his attention. But it hadn't been. Something about her had seemed familiar.

He leaned in, as if it would help him hear. It didn't. He watched as she checked in with the guy, asked him a couple of questions, then gestured to one of the other surfers to come over.

What *was* it about her that seemed so familiar?

He lost sight of her for a moment, as she slipped off her board and dived under, just as a wave crested and crashed over her board.

Broken Nose Bloke was now being towed to shore by another surfer.

He hadn't realised he'd been holding his breath until the redhead resurfaced with a blonde who, with the help of the other surfers, was soon loaded onto her board and also towed in.

Noah's brain kicked into gear. Weaving elements of his old life into his new one was the only way he could see this working. 'C'mon, girls. You up for a run? Who can make it to the Jeep to grab Uncle Noah's medical bag first?'

Amidst a chorus of 'Me! Me!' and 'I can do it!' they ran.

Noah jogged into the surf and began to do the one thing he knew he was good at. Practising medicine.

Noah had done a quick reset of the lad's nose almost before he'd even hit the shore. Now that his nieces had returned with his medical bag, he popped a temporary bandage over the nasty gash on the young man's cheek. As predicted, it was from his board fin—the laser-sharp steering device. He'd definitely need stitches.

Noah felt a punch of pride that his nieces, who had virtually grown up in the medical clinic his sister ran—he checked himself, *had run*—were more fascinated than grossed out, and were now standing by waiting to help with the next patient.

Noah looked out to the water just as the surfers were pulling the board with the blonde woman on it to shore. Walking alongside the board was the redhead. She was giving the blonde a sternal rub.

Interesting… Not your bog-standard first aid knowledge.

'Come on, Kylie. This isn't the way this is going to end. Not today. Not on my watch.'

Her cheeks were streaked with tears, or maybe droplets from the ocean. Difficult to tell. Her expression was dark. She knew the young woman's name, so chances were high they were friends. Although there was a bit of an age gap. Mother? No. Not that much. Didn't matter. Age-guessing wasn't his priority.

'What's wrong with her?' one of the crowd asked.

'She's unconscious,' the redhead answered. 'I'm not sure if she's inhaled water or been knocked on the head by the board.' She did one more sternal rub, then pressed her fingers to Kylie's throat and paled. 'No pulse.'

No pulse indicated that she'd inhaled water and had begun to drown. She needed CPR straight away. Water blocking the airway meant no oxygen, and if that were the case it was possible she'd been without oxygen for several minutes now. Too long meant permanent brain damage or worse.

'Can someone take the leash off?' Noah asked

as he waded in and grabbed one end of Kylie's board, easily hoisting her towards the safety of the beach. Two other surf dudes had the other end, while the auburn-haired woman began to shoo people back.

When they'd set the board down, Noah did a lightning-fast visual check. The sternal rub had produced some foam at her mouth. A good sign, in this case. Her body was expelling water. Forty seconds underwater after an involuntary inhalation was enough to drown an adult. Twenty seconds could take a child's life.

Reflexively, Noah glanced round and checked that the girls were well clear of the surf. It was receding. He didn't know the cove intimately, but he knew enough about tides to know there was a tug to the waves, and those precious little humans simply did not have the strength to fight it.

'She needs CPR! Clear the space,' the woman demanded.

Noah took a step forward.

'I said clear the space,' she repeated firmly.

Their eyes met and locked. It couldn't have been for more than a second that their gazes meshed, maybe less, but something about the passage of time changed in that instant.

Some people said fear made time appear to stand still, while others claimed it could be anything new—making the brain strain to register and understand what was happening. In medical terms, it was the cerebral cortex making a faulty overestimation of the duration of a stimuli connected to the fight-or-flight response. He didn't feel like fighting. And he wasn't, despite her request, going to move.

There was another option. One his sister would've pounced on because it would explain why his heart was crashing against his chest. Why he could feel his pulse in his throat. An oxytocin surge. Love at first sight.

He blinked the thought away.

Something at first sight, maybe.

Recognition?

He *saw* himself in her forest-green eyes. Not literally, of course, but…

Hand on heart, he could see a version of himself deep within the flecks of her gold and green irises. Felt an affinity shift between them… energy syncing with the sparks flashing in her pupils.

He had no idea how he knew—*déjà-vu?*—but he knew that, like him, she had grounded her life in facts, only to have her reality upended by one of life's blunt U-turns. A traumatic event had destroyed the path she'd prepared for herself. A path as straight and well-laid-out as his had been. She was, in short, a kindred spirit.

Where the hell did he know her from?

The moment ended as quickly as it had begun.

'I'm a doctor,' they both said at the same time.

Again, their eyes met and locked, this time with a shared understanding. They could both help Kylie.

'Rebecca.' She pointed at herself.

'Noah.'

There was another microsecond of connection. More complex this time. Something that ingrained itself in him on a cellular level. An exchange of energy that clarified something they both knew to be true: Kylie's life was in their hands.

Together they dropped to their knees beside Kylie. Rebecca spoke as she pressed two fingers together and made a quick swoop of Kylie's mouth, clearing it of the foam.

'She wanted to do one last run. She was overtired, but against my advice went out anyway. Broken Nose Bloke dropped in on her wave. His board clipped hers. She went under and didn't resurface for a good ninety seconds. She's a strong swimmer but she was caught off guard.'

There was no anger or frustration in her voice. Just facts. The perfect 'doctor' tone.

In another textbook re-enactment of her medical training, Rebecca kept saying her patient's name. 'Kylie? Kylie, can you hear me?' No response. 'We're here with you, Kylie.'

His eyes snapped to hers. How had they become a 'we'?

'I can't do this alone,' she said.

The words exploded in him like a grenade.

She had more strength of character than he did.

A couple of years back, when his sister and her husband had been doing their wills, she'd suggested he take some time to think about whether he really was happy to be named their guardian. He'd been newly single, and his sister had her doubts. He'd struggle to do it on his own, she'd warned him. She and her husband had trouble balancing everything, and they were a team.

'Don't be ridiculous,' he'd retorted, grabbing the paperwork and signing it. *'It's not as if it'll ever happen,'* he'd said.

Another grenade went off.

It was something he knew to do in his operating theatre—to expect the unexpected. But somehow he hadn't trained himself to brace for it in real life.

'You okay?'

Rebecca was looking at him as if she was reading his thoughts. He nodded, annoyed with himself that he'd faltered, even for a nanosecond. Each fraction of time was precious to this woman. So they got to work.

With Noah's help, Rebecca rolled the young woman onto her back, still on the surfboard— a better surface for compressions than the sand.

'I'll do rescue breaths—you do compressions.' She pointed at her arms as a signal that hers were tired after swimming into shore.

No ego. She earned another notch of his respect. Some people might have insisted on performing the 'glory' job. She clearly knew the real glory came from getting it right.

Without waiting for an answer, she tilted Kylie's chin and head backwards, to keep the airway as wide open as possible. A swathe of auburn hair swept down as she leant forward.

Noah's fingers twitched with an absurd desire to push it across her shoulder to her back. He cursed himself for the lack of focus, tugged his phone out of his pocket and got one of his nieces to hold it so he could get the staff at the clinic to prep a room for them.

The most up-to-date CPR advice was to forgo the rescue breaths, but in the case of drowning a handful of breaths could make the critical difference. Rebecca gave Kylie five rescue breaths.

Noah had already woven his fingers together, one palm over the other, and as soon as she'd finished he began compressions.

As he neared the end of the minute-long cycle, Rebecca began counting out loud. 'One-eighteen, one-nineteen, one-twenty.' She leant forward as he held his hands up and gave two more rescue breaths.

He did another sixty compressions. This time, before Rebecca could count him out, Kylie lurched forward, and the water that had been trapped in her lungs began to be expelled. They swiftly shifted her into the recovery position as the crowd around them burst into spontaneous applause, complete with a round of back-slapping and hugs and *Thank Gods*.

There were a couple of foil blankets in his kit but, not wanting to put them directly against Kylie's skin, Noah pulled his shirt off and tucked it around her shoulders.

When he looked up again, Rebecca's gaze wasn't on his face.

CHAPTER THREE

REBECCA BIT DOWN on the inside of her cheek so hard she drew blood. It was the only way she could stop herself from reaching across and touching Noah to make sure he wasn't a mirage.

A man this perfect couldn't be mortal. Could he? Who even *had* a physique like that? Certainly not her ex. It wasn't gym-built. No. That kind of beauty was… It was… He was…

Not. Available.

'Did I ace the wave?' Kylie's weak voice broke through the silence and, mercifully, ended Rebecca's staring contest with Noah's pin-up-ready torso.

'You were perfect,' Rebecca whispered.

And then, of course, her eyes met Noah's.

He arched an inquisitive eyebrow. She practically felt his gaze drop down to her lips…just as she was licking them. His eyes pinged back to hers and her body lit up as if she were a one-woman advertisement for holiday romances.

Rather than launch herself at him, she made herself focus on Kylie, even though her body was practically vibrating with a life-force she'd never known she possessed.

Was this what living outside her comfort zone was meant to make her feel like? Charged like a thousand-watt bulb?

After checking that Kylie's skin wasn't cold, or tinted with the tell-tale blue of hypothermia, she had checked for any unusual abdominal swellings and made sure she felt well enough to travel. Then they'd bundled the lad with the broken nose and Kylie into the Jeep Noah's little girls had guided them to.

All this while she had been averting her gaze from Noah's chest. And his back. And his sexy arm tattoos. But most of all his face. Apart from the fact he was like vitamins for the eyes, she couldn't shake the feeling of having met him before.

Like a soulmate.

Rebecca kept one hand on Kylie's pulse and, as she was now seated in the back of the Jeep, her eyes on what she could see of Noah's profile. The man was clearly off-limits, but no matter how much she chastised herself she couldn't stop herself from staring.

This was a serious moth-to-the-flame situation. Obvious enough to draw Kylie's attention.

Because, even though she was exhausted, and still experiencing a jagged-sounding cough, she had enough energy to start whisper-singing. 'Rebecca and Noah, sitting in a tree…'

Rebecca gently pressed a finger to her friend's lips and, through a smirk of her own, intoned, 'Hush. Save your energy. You've been through a serious trauma.'

Which, to be fair, she had. If they'd been at the last hospital where she'd worked, before she'd decamped to Cornwall, she'd be demanding a full neurological work-up and scans galore. Of her lungs, her stomach, her brain. A lot could go wrong when you were without oxygen—but, seeing as Kylie was well enough to tease her, she was pretty sure twenty-four hours of observation would conclude that she'd had a very near miss.

She gave her friend's hand a squeeze and smoothed her blonde hair back from her forehead. Poor love. How terrifying.

And then she went right back to staring at Noah.

As the vehicle wove beneath the canopy of thick jungle foliage, Rebecca tried to figure out what the universe was doing by gifting her someone she couldn't have. It seemed mean.

Anyway… She doubted she could handle getting naked in front of someone who looked *that* divine, let alone orgasm in front of him.

She wasn't exactly a supermodel. Plus-sizes and comfort clothes were her normal apparel. And scrubs. In fact, mostly scrubs. This whole 'swimsuit as daywear' thing was only because she knew she'd never see anyone she met here again.

And why was she even thinking about things like that? It wasn't as if they were on their way to his secret mountain lair, where he would have his wicked way to her. This presumably married father of two was driving them to a medical clinic to check her friend hadn't sustained brain damage.

And yet…

Every time her eyes connected with Noah's it felt as if he'd zapped her with something. A live current. When their hands had accidentally brushed against each other's when they'd loaded Kylie into his very fancy Jeep spontaneous combustion had seemed a genuine possibility.

Being the gifted flirt she wasn't, she'd done the sexiest thing possible and asked him if he was happy for Kylie to throw up in the back of this vehicle. Because, if she wasn't mistaken, it still had that new car smell. Her ex would've called an ambulance to do the job. He was very precious about his vehicles. Too bad he hadn't felt that way about her heart.

Noah had given her a look that spoke volumes.

A person's life trumps that new car smell.

And that had set a whole new raft of butterflies into flight in her tummy.

Unlike her ex, who had become a doctor because that was what generations of the men in his family before him had done, Noah seemed to have arrived on earth pre-programmed to want to fix what was broken.

As if he was reading her mind, his eyes met hers in the rear-view mirror and he gave her a tight nod of affirmation.

Her heart skipped a beat. And then a few more. She fanned herself with the back of her hand. Who needed AEDs when you had a Noah? He'd done more to her nervous system in the span of ten minutes than David had ever done over the course of five entire years. Had she ever even known what love was?

The thought threatened to crack her in half. She quickly corseted it and returned to her safe place: pragmatics.

Regardless of all these carnal thoughts and feelings, Noah was no-go territory. Unlike her ex's new wife, Rebecca didn't stray into territory that wasn't hers. She knew how deep those wounds cut.

Besides, Noah was literally perfect, so even the idea that he would consider cheating on his trim blonde wife with Rebecca—a taller than

average 'big-boned' girl from the West Country, with a dedication to spreadsheeting—was
ludicrous. Especially not with two gorgeous
inky-haired chatterbox daughters who, at present, were sitting up front on the bench seat asking Broken Nose Bloke—aka Mack Redding,
a surfer and plumber from Brisbane—if, when
he had stitches, which in their estimation was a
sure thing, they could watch.

He gave a quick glance at Noah, as if to say
Is that okay? Noah rolled his eyes and nodded.
Mack said it was the least he could do. 'How
about you do them for me, little ladies? Which
one of you are up for it?' he asked.

They dissolved into gales of laughter.

Rebecca had done about a million stitches in
her time. She was about to volunteer when Mack
flicked his thumb back in her direction.

'Can Red do them?' Mack asked Noah. 'No
offence, Doc, but she's got smaller hands.'

He dropped her a wink and made a noise Rebecca was fairly certain was meant to be flirta-
tious. But, as much as she was trying to follow
the universe's hints, he was definitely not her
type.

Noah spread his palms wide against the steering wheel, then tightened them round the leather.
Rebecca saw what Mack couldn't. Those were
surgeon's hands. Or maybe… Was he jealous?

No. He was married. It was more likely that he was annoyed this guy couldn't tell one quality set of doctor's hands from another.

It suddenly struck her that she hadn't asked Noah what his connection to the clinic was. She knew the one he'd mentioned. Simply called The Island Clinic, it was on the edge of a village halfway between the cove where they'd just been and the much more heavily frequented surfer beach adjacent to Rebecca's resort. She rode one of the resort bicycles to the village every day, to a place that made amazing coffee and even more delicious fruit smoothies.

And then, as her eyes connected with Noah's in the rear-view mirror and his frown dug a furrow between his eyebrows, she knew exactly where she'd seen him before.

'You're Mr Guava, Lime and Pineapple Crush!'

She clapped her hand over her mouth, horrified that the words had leapt out like that.

She'd told Kylie all about him. The man who appeared like clockwork at the juice bar at eleven every morning, wearing black scrubs and a frown. He was never rude. And it wasn't an angry frown. It was more…haunted. As if he'd seen things in the operating theatre no mortal should ever have to witness.

She bit down on her lip as his eyes bored into hers until the horn from a passing car sounded.

He returned his gaze to the road—but not for long. They flicked back and forth between the road and her as his mind visibly whirred, trying to connect the dots.

'What?' Kylie squawked. 'Your sexy surly doc gave me the kiss of life?'

'Er… No. I did that,' she whispered making a hand gesture so Kylie would keep the volume down.

'Phew! I mean, not that he's gross—he's totally hot. But I'm obvs taken.'

'He's also driving this vehicle,' Rebecca growled. 'Shh.'

Kylie smirked, and in a loud clear voice said, 'Get in there, girl!'

Noah's eyes snapped to Rebecca's in the rearview mirror. He wasn't smiling.

A flush of embarrassment swept up her neck, illuminating her cheeks like a harvest moon. Just last night she had—very uncharacteristically—brought herself to orgasm thinking about him. Her face went a darker shade of crimson. She never did that sort of thing. One minute she'd been thinking about smoothies, and the next she'd been turning Mr Guava, Lime and Pineapple Crush into a smooth talker who knew how to slip a girl's sundress off her shoulders with a heavenly effect on her erogenous zones.

This was humiliation of the highest order. Thank God she hadn't mentioned *that* to Kylie.

Kylie tried to press herself up, but began coughing so hard that Rebecca got her to lie back on her side. Flirting, or whatever this was—angry staring?—while ignoring your friend, who might be suffering from dry drowning, wasn't really the sort of incident she'd like hung out to dry in front of the medical board.

Well, Your Honour. You see... There was this super-hot guy I kept seeing when I was sitting outside this bijou medical clinic that, in a tropical way, reminded me of the sort of thing I once wanted to run, before my fiancé stomped all over my heart and destroyed our shared hopes and dreams by getting another woman pregnant with twins and moving to London to be with them.

Sorry, what? What was I doing outside the medical clinic? I suppose you could call it loitering with intent. Was I hurt? No. I mean, apart from the heartbreak side of things. But, look... The truth is, I was deciding whether or not to beg the people at the clinic for a job, so I could start my life over again here in Bali rather than move back to the UK and face my demons head-on, but—like I said—there was this super-hot doctor who gave me tingles even thinking about—

You what, now? Yes, that's right. I sat outside

the clinic for several days. At the juice bar, actu-
ally. Why did I stop? My friend Kylie made me
go surfing with her, because she said the juice
bar wasn't helping me find my Zen.

It had seemed such a good idea at the time.
Dreaming about a future so entirely different
from the GP surgery she and her ex had planned
on opening. But she'd kept seeing this glow-
ering, gorgeous man hunk, and the thought of
working with someone so…so scrumptiously
scowly—Heathcliff *sur la mer*—seemed bor-
dering on insanity.

He gave her butterflies. Everywhere. In *pub-*
lic.

Kylie had decided for her in the end, announc-
ing that men who frowned when ordering a
drink that sounded like the punchline to a joke
were not suitable rebound material. And 'jumping back on the horse' was something Kylie had
been actively encouraging her to do since the
day they'd met. With a happy go-lucky type.
Like Mack.

Rebecca glanced at the surfer, who was now
delighting the little girls by making faces.

A sigh hoisted up her shoulders, then wilted
them.

Now that she knew Noah was married, she
thought that at least she'd spared herself the humiliation of asking him for a job. Because work-

ing with this walking, talking, surgical example
of everything she'd ever wanted—apart from the
frowning—would have been torture.

How could she not have recognised him on
the beach?

*Maybe because he was half-naked and about
a thousand times more gorgeous than he looked
in his black scrubs, you idiot.*

Plus, he'd been smiling when she'd spotted
him with the girls. So she wasn't a complete
idiot. The smile had changed his entire aura.
And it had been a beautiful thing to behold.

'Mr Guava, Lime and Pineapple Crush, eh?'
Mack mimicked when he caught Rebecca staring again. He obviously thought Rebecca was
backing the wrong horse. 'Sounds like someone
fancies someone else.' He made some *boom-
chica-boom* noises, instantly regretting the im-
pact the movement had on his face.

'Ooh!' The little girls twisted round in their
seats in tandem, to stare at Rebecca.

'No! No one fancies anyone. I just—' She
took in a shaky breath and continued in a voice
that was so British she was surprised the words
didn't etch themselves into the windows. 'I happen to have noticed that Noah buys juice. That
is all.'

She glanced towards the rear-view mirror
again and cringed. Noah was suppressing a

smile. Did he *like* it that she'd noticed him at the juice bar?

Stop it! You cannot be a lust monster. Not with a married father of two.

He gave his chin a rub and said, 'Perhaps the girls will run over and get you a turmeric, ginger and coconut water while my cousin does the stitches. You might've seen her down at the beach? She's waiting for us at the clinic.'

Each word tumbled through her as if she was a pinball machine. He knew *her* drink, too.

'What about me?' whined Mack. 'I'm thirsty, too.'

Wait a minute… Cousin? Was the blonde she'd seen at the beach his *cousin*?

Her stomach swirled and lifted in a pirouette of joy.

'Get in there, girlfriend.' Kylie poked her with a finger.

'No way,' Rebecca whispered. 'I have to stay with you.'

Not that she could ever look Noah in the eye again. Not since she'd remembered…you know… Okay, fine. It had been a double orgasm. Fictional Noah was a terrific lover. But real-life Noah had two little girls who had to have a mother out there somewhere.

Kylie narrowed her eyes and tried to pull her backpack from Rebecca's lap. 'I'm going to text the Surf God. He can sit with me.' She flicked her fingers at Rebecca. 'You get on with crushing some tropical fruits.'

Just as Rebecca was going to begin a lecture on all the reasons why prancing off to a juice bar with a married stranger was ridiculous, Noah shifted down a gear and swung the Jeep into an alley away from the bustling high street.

At the back of the clinic, two enormous carved wooden doors were opened by a pair of uniformed men waiting in a small sentry house.

'Blimey, mate.' Mack climbed out of the Jeep and whistled. 'This place is a bit of a surprise.'

Mack wasn't kidding.

For starters, the clinic building was about a thousand times larger than it appeared from the front. Perhaps it was because the sun had hit that magical hour where everything was bathed in a diaphanous cloud of gold. Or maybe it was because this was like no clinic she'd ever seen before. It might also be because the man who had turned her body into a hotbed of molten hormones was looking directly at her with an intensity that demanded an honest reaction.

Whatever it was, Rebecca felt as if she'd entered an entirely different universe.

The modest stone wall and human-sized red door she'd stared at from the juice bar clearly hid a Tardis. Here, round the back, verdant palms arched over an enormous drive that led into a flourishing and expansive tropical garden, complete with soothing water features and a beautifully tiled infinity pool.

Nooks and crannies were carved into the bougainvillea-covered stone walls. Thick teak shelves supported shrines bedecked with offerings of fresh flowers and fruit. Individual villas were dotted about the gardens, each made from traditional materials in keeping with the large central building.

Noah was out of the driver's seat and opening the back door just as she leant forward to push the door open. Like a tropically dressed knight in shining armour, Noah somehow foresaw her lack of balance and scooped one arm under her legs and the other round her back so that she tumbled into his chest.

Rather than set her on the ground at once, or make an unfunny joke about her weight like her ex would have done, Noah continued to hold her, and for a curiously private-feeling moment it was as if the only people in the world who existed were the two of them.

His eyes—squid-ink-black from a distance—were actually more like lapis lazuli, gem-like in their blue-black ability to reflect light. He had freckles on his nose. A light smattering. She'd never known freckles seem masculine before.

All of him was, actually. He was made of muscle and strength, without seeming as hard and inaccessible as that frown he sometimes wore.

A ripple of heat ran through her as his fingers shifted against her thigh. This was far superior to the fantasy she'd conjured up last night. His warm skin glowed with the scents she had come to associate with the island. Coconut. Sea-salted air. Lemongrass and pepper.

She met his gaze again, and in that instant a miracle occurred. She felt feminine for the first time in she didn't know how long. Possibly ever.

She wasn't a tiny woman—something her ex had never let her forget whenever she'd hinted that she might wear heels to an event. She didn't know why she'd bothered. It wasn't *her* fault he couldn't make six foot even in boots. She'd always worn ballet pumps in the end.

Relationships were meant to be about compromise, right? But maybe that had been part of the problem. Perhaps they'd pushed the definition of compromise into territory more akin to acquiescence. Pushed it to the point where neither of them had ended up happy.

Noah didn't strike her as a man who would make her wear ballet flats to avoid bruising his ego. Then again, Noah would be able to rest his chin on her head even if she wore heels.

'Oh, for the love of Pete!' Kylie was crouching in the doorframe, waiting to climb out. 'Will you two stop staring at one another and move, so I can get out of this caboose and back to the resort?'

Noah released Rebecca to the ground with an awkward clearing of the throat, and when he went to lift Kylie out was met with a feminist lecture on how she didn't need a man to help her even if she had been half dead—

'Whoa!'

Rebecca and Noah lunged for Kylie as she pitched forward.

'Maybe I could do with a little bit of help.'

'You and me both, mate,' Mack said, rounding the corner of the Jeep.

They turned around to see that his temporary bandage was soaked through, and that what blood was left in his face had drained away.

'Good heavens, Noah! Did you get into a fist fight down at the beach?'

The beautiful blonde from the beach appeared on the wide porch at the back of the main building with a wheelchair.

'Girls. It's time for your supper and then baths, all right? I'll be over to the villa to help in a few moments.' She turned her gaze back to Noah, then shrugged. 'I guess I don't have to ask if you had a fun time at the beach, then, do I?'

A flurry of motion ensued.

Rebecca received a sharp 'get in there' elbow in her ribs from Kylie, just before the blonde scuttled the wheelchair down to them and introduced herself as Mel McKindry, Noah's cousin.

Kylie gave Rebecca a look.

Rebecca turned fuchsia.

Noah grabbed the tablet that had been on the wheelchair seat and started furiously typing.

Mel beamed at Rebecca. 'New friend of Noah's?' She flicked her gaze at her cousin, still tapping his tablet. 'Well done, mate. It's about time you brought someone back.'

If Rebecca wasn't mistaken, Noah growled.

Before either of them could explain, Mel called out to a colleague to bring another wheelchair and then shot a series of rapid-fire questions at the lot of them—medically based—while somehow managing to pull Rebecca's history from her as well.

Her nationality—British—the amount of time she'd been in Bali—a fortnight—whether she planned to stay—that was up in the air right now—and what sort of medicine she practised—trained as a paediatric surgeon then retrained as a GP.

'So that's what you're doing now? Working in general practice back in England?'

'Um…' Her eyes flicked to Noah's. 'Not exactly.'

'She's single, doesn't have a job, and is currently at one of life's more significant crossroads,' Kylie supplied, with a beam and a knowing wink at Noah. Rebecca jabbed her in the ribs only to receive a wounded, '*What?* It's the truth. Oh!' She brightened. 'And she has an open-ended ticket that she needs to change tomorrow. Just saying…'

As if Noah's cousin had received all the information she required, she beamed at Mack. 'I've got just the doctor to sort out your stitches, mate.' An artfully tattooed black-haired doctor who looked as if he spent most of his spare time in a boxing ring appeared and wheeled Mack off.

'Well, then…' Mel gave Kylie's hand a pat. 'I think I'll leave you under my *single* cousin Noah's care, with Rebecca accompanying you to ensure you feel comfortable with a male doctor, yeah?' To Rebecca she added, 'If you're happy staying in your swimsuit, please do. Otherwise I'm sure Noah could set you up with some scrubs.'

She gave Kylie a complicit wink, as if her almost drowning had all been part of an elaborate plan to get the two doctors to meet one another.

Rebecca managed to surface from her mortification for long enough to absorb the fact that Dr Noah Cameron was single.

Kylie hummed a happy little tune as Noah wheeled her up a ramp and into the main building.

For what appeared to be a simple tourist clinic from the outside, The Island Clinic had a lot of bells and whistles. And, twenty minutes in, Rebecca was pleased to see Noah was making use of most of them. He'd earned Rebecca's approval by ordering a number of scans, as well as running several simple neurological tests to ensure the absence of oxygen hadn't had any derogatory effect on Kylie.

Later, as the cicadas took up their night song and wafts of citronella drifted in with the breeze billowing the mosquito netting on the windows, Rebecca was struck by how ultra-romantic this setting could be. Which she took as her cue to get a move on. If she was looking at hospitals as romantic it was definitely time to leave.

'I'll be in tomorrow morning, once you've had a second round of neuro tests,' she told Kylie.

Kylie groaned. 'Don't go! Who am I going to talk to?'

Rebecca glanced around the room. There was a shelf with some well-worn books on it. Romances, from the looks of things. 'Here. Read one of these.'

She handed her a book, which Kylie refused to take.

'I bet you were a really bossy doctor back home,' Kylie whined. 'Why can't I go back to the resort and show the Surf God there's nothing wrong with me?'

'Maybe because it's an all-female resort and you need to rest?'

'You're not a nice doctor.' Kylie pouted.

'And you're a terrible patient,' Rebecca countered with a grin.

'If you won't listen to the lovely doctor, you'll have to listen to the grumpy one.'

Noah's deep Australian-accented voice came from the doorway, once again sending his words ricocheting through Rebecca's nervous system.

Lovely?

She felt like the ugly duckling on the brink of turning into a swan. What would happen if he spoke actual *sexy* words to her? She might lose control all together. She blushed remembering the moment when, alone in her bed, she had. And that had just been *thinking* about him.

'I don't think it'll surprise you to hear that we want to keep you in overnight for observation.' Noah gave the doorframe a knock, as if to say the matter was set in stone.

Rebecca smirked.

Kylie growled. 'I won't stay unless Rebecca stays, too.'

Rebecca glared at Kylie. If she hadn't nearly

drowned today, she would definitely have hit her with a pillow. She couldn't stay here! Not with Dr Dangerously Delicious within arm's reach. *And his two perfect children.*

There was definitely a story there. One that mysteriously involved his cousin wanting to set him up with a complete stranger.

Noah's eyes flicked between the two of them, his eyebrows quirking as he tried to puzzle out which way this conversation was going to go.

Mel appeared in the doorway and did a lightning-fast reading of the scene.

'Hi, gang. Those scrubs suit you, Rebecca. They really bring out the green in your eyes. Don't they Noah?' She didn't wait for an answer. 'Hey… They're just about to bring supper round to all the patients. Kylie, I was hoping I might trade you one Rebecca for one of these…' She stepped to the side and in walked the Surf God.

Kylie squealed, then coughed, then clapped her hands and scooted over in her bed so that there was room for her holiday beau. A space he promptly filled.

'Well, then…' Mel grinned. 'I guess that leaves us three free to discuss who's going to take over from me when I head back to Sydney.'

CHAPTER FOUR

'SO...' REBECCA WAS staring doggedly at the menu the clinic's restaurant staff had just provided. 'What do you recommend?'

Leaving before my cousin commandeers your entire life!

Noah swallowed the words before they could gain traction. It was an unkind thought and it wasn't even aimed at Rebecca—a woman he would definitely be trying to charm into staying if this were a different time and a different place. A time when all the responsibility he'd had in life was his job and sending money here to the clinic to assuage his guilty conscience.

But it wasn't. It was here and now, and his guilty conscience had been pulled up sharply, forcing him to fulfil promises he'd never imagined would become his reality. Mostly because he'd never thought of a world without his sister in it. But that was the reality. One he and the girls had been left to survive.

Despite his newly established routine of perching on one of the kitchen stools in his sister's house—one ear on the girls' room, one on his pager, with a stack of patient reports as his reading material—his cousin had steered Noah and Rebecca out here to the courtyard restaurant to 'discuss employment possibilities', only for her to remember she'd promised the girls she'd help them with their baths.

He wasn't an idiot. She was obviously trying to set him up with Rebecca despite the spectacularly bad timing. Or because of it? He didn't know any more.

A few months ago his life had been as predictable as sunshine in Bali. Hell, a few *years* ago his life had been as predictable. Work, eat, sleep, repeat. The odd girlfriend had been factored into his schedule—right up until she figured out he wasn't going to propose or start a family, in an abbreviated version of what had happened to him and Alice—his med school girlfriend—after eight years of going out together. They'd been all work and some play, and he'd thought that was enough.

When his mum had died Alice had finally called his bluff after his promises that 'it'll happen one day'.

It had. But not with him. She was now happily married, had three cute little kids, and was living out in Perth with a husband who prized family time above all else.

Since then he hadn't bothered with false promises. As a result, his relationships were short and mostly sweet. When you dated in your thirties it was best to be honest with women, because he knew for them the biological clock ticked louder and faster. Now he was forty-one, and effectively a single dad...

In theory, he wanted a soulmate and children. But for reasons he couldn't explain he just hadn't felt that 'click' his sister had spoken about when she'd met her husband. That magic moment when she'd known she was ready to start a family.

'Anything I'd regret not trying?' Rebecca tapped her menu, reminding him that she had asked for a recommendation.

He rubbed his face. He was making a proper hash of things. Rebecca was one of those 'league of her own' women. Someone who deserved the cream of the dating crop. Not an emotionally unavailable orthopaedic surgeon trying to figure out whether to stay here or pack up his nieces and head back to Sydney.

And just like that his long 'To Do' list reared its ugly head. He'd have to sell his condo if they moved. Too much glass. Too many sharp corners. Not enough bedrooms. Was it even near a school? He had no idea.

'Am I to take your silence as a no?' Rebecca asked, bemused.

'No, sorry. Everything's good.'

Get your act together, man!

'I was just—' His eyes snagged on her full mouth again, almost expecting the peek of her tongue as it swept along her bottom lip.

'Distracted?' She filled in for him.

His eyes flicked back up to hers. Beautiful. Calm in a crisis. A loyal friend. She was someone he could see himself having a kid with.

What? Where the hell had that come from?

He picked up his menu, cutting off his view of her. 'Let's take a look.'

The words blurred in front of his eyes. He owed this woman more than sub-par chitchat. He also owed his cousin the indulgence of thinking she'd done the right thing by pairing him up with someone so he wouldn't feel abandoned when she headed back to Oz.

As interfering as she could be, Mel had been an epic heroine these past couple of months.

Keeping his father and his third wife busy enough to ensure they rarely crossed paths with him at the funeral had been just one of Mel's superpowers. The fact his father had shown up at all was galling. Yeah, okay, he had been Indah's biological dad, and his, but had he ever really been a father to them?

How Mel had bundled him back to Oz without one fight erupting between father and son had been little short of a miracle.

It had been hard to imagine a man as flawed as his father witnessing a purification ceremony. The memory of it churned in his gut. As if his sister had needed any improvement. Or her husband. They'd been the good ones. The kind ones. The generous ones. Probably like Rebecca. After all, how many women would sit here with a man who seemed to have had all of the words he knew sucked out of him?

'Would you suggest a starter?' Rebecca prompted now, with saintlike patience. 'Or go straight to the main course?'

He looked at her then. Really looked at her. She was a beautiful woman. She had a glow about her that wasn't just aesthetic. It spoke of a personal warmth. A strength of character. If he'd been back in Sydney, maybe that 'click' would've latched into place...

But he wasn't, and it wouldn't.

And all she wants is a recommendation for what to eat so she can get the heck out of here, you idiot.

'I always start with the satay,' he said lamely. Everyone started with the satay.

C'mon, man! Your mother was Indonesian. You grew up with this food. He'd also grown up with an Australian father who'd insisted upon a 'proper Sunday lunch' every week after church. The same man who had preached loyalty as the most essential of traits, only to be revealed as a serial philanderer. Even when his mum had been dying of cancer. Class in a glass, his father. Class in a glass. Somehow what he lacked in fidelity he made up for in charm. A real modern-day Casanova.

At least his second wife had told him where to stuff it. It'd be interesting to see how long the third one hung in there. She'd not looked all that happy when they'd come over last month. Then again, it had been a funeral.

Rebecca generously pretended they were having a lively conversation and soldiered on. 'I adore a good satay. Is it just me, or does the Balinese one have an extra kick? Spicy...'

She ducked her head so that her eyes met his, and just like that they shared one of those jolts of electric current that seemed to pass between them every time their gazes intersected. As quickly as their eyes meshed they were torn apart, hers dropping back to her menu, his lifting up to the thatched palm roof of the outdoor dining area.

Was she feeling it, too? This...*connection*?

He'd had forty-one years to feel the 'click' with a woman and it was happening now. When his life was chaos. It didn't make sense. Bones, joints, ligaments and tendons... Those were the things he'd dedicated his professional career to. Those made sense. They didn't come with double meanings or hidden subtext. They were ripped, torn, broken, bruised. Things he could repair. Orthopaedics was straightforward. Honest.

Was his response to Rebecca an honest one, or a panicked reaction to his new circumstances?

All work and no play...

He crushed his sister's oft-repeated words in his hand.

Rebecca looked at him, startled. She set her menu down, shifting her chair away from the table. 'I'm going to be honest with you. I am getting the distinct impression you have somewhere else you need to be.'

The gold flecks in her eyes flared in the candlelight. Her top teeth took purchase on her bottom lip. A current of electricity ran through his veins.

'No. Please stay. I'm being a jackass. You've done nothing wrong.'

Her skin turned a deep shade of pink, exposing a side of her he hadn't seen before. It was less protected than the version he'd first met.

Raw, almost. He related to it. This glimpse of vulnerability.

What if you show her you're as vulnerable as she is?

And what if he tore off his shirt, beat his chest and admitted that he was clinging to every cell of inner alpha male he could? Because if he didn't, it'd be clear for all to see that he didn't have a clue what he was doing, and that for the first time in his life he wished he had a loved one by his side who knew him inside and out. Someone who could assure him he could do this. Someone like Rebecca.

After a moment's silence she squinted at him. 'I might be humiliating myself here, but do you get the feeling that your cousin is trying to set us up?'

And just like that the tension in the air dissipated.

Noah burst out laughing. 'She's not exactly subtle, is she?'

Rebecca shook her head, then scrunched her features up before releasing them into an expression he hadn't seen on her before. Feistiness. It suited her.

'Shame,' she said, almost wistfully.

'What is?'

'That you're not my type.'

He was shocked to feel his heart drop down

to his gut. He wasn't in any place to be with anyone, but it stung that she wouldn't even give him a chance.

Before he could respond she continued, 'You're all gorgeous and broody and…' She waved her hands in front of him, as if that finished off the definition. 'Suffice it to say you're not someone I'd normally be set up with.'

He sat back and rubbed his jaw. 'I'm not sure if I'm meant to take that as a compliment or not.'

She shrugged. 'It's just a statement of fact.'

He smiled. He liked facts. He also liked honesty. So he did what he should've done the moment his cousin had left them alone. He said, 'I have a pretty complicated situation right now.'

She nodded, as if it wasn't a surprise to her.

He continued, 'My sister Indah was killed a couple of months ago. Both her and her husband.'

Rebecca gasped and pressed her hands to her chest. 'The two little girls…?'

He nodded. 'They're hers. *Were* hers,' he corrected reluctantly. 'I'm their guardian now… so you've caught me in the middle of deciding whether to stay here and run the clinic, which was basically my sister's thing, or whether to find a nanny in Sydney and go back to the life I know there.'

'Which is…?'

'I'm chief orthopaedic surgeon at Sydney Orthopaedics.' Getting that job had been his goal. He'd attained it just a few short months before Indah had been killed.

'Gosh.' She blew out a big breath, as if living his experiences herself. 'That's a big life-change. And I thought mine was big.'

He gave her a curious look.

She pointed at her ring finger. 'That had something on it a few months ago.'

'You broke it off?'

She winced. 'Well, technically, yes—but the fact he was in love with someone else who was bearing his child made it feel like less of a win.'

'Ouch.'

'You can say that again.' She took a sip of her water, then decisively put the glass down. 'Anyway. Rather than grieving for the family I don't have right now, I'm trying to look at it as a close shave with the wrong gene pool. It's nothing like what you're going through.'

It was, actually. They'd both been hurt. Deeply so. And they were both doing their best to find a future with some joy in it.

'I actually think we have more in common than you think.' He put on his scowling face. 'Apart from my broodiness, obviously.'

She laughed, then gave him a sidelong look. 'What on earth do we have in common?'

'Neither of us is living the life we thought we would be.'

She lifted her glass to his and they clinked.

'Look,' she said, after a moment's companionable silence, 'I don't know if this was a date set-up or a job set-up, but please don't think you have to ask me to work here. I'm pretty sure there are plenty of Indonesian doctors who would be thrilled to work in a beautiful place like this.'

'Most of our staff are local,' he admitted. 'Although, saying that, the clinic runs almost like two clinics. We serve the tourist population, but we also like to offer free medical care and more complex treatments to the poorer local population, courtesy of specialist surgeons who fly in to donate their time and expertise. So we actually need a mix of staff. Local and international. Do you know any languages?'

She answered without pausing to think about it. 'French and Spanish.'

Impressive. And useful. He should hire her. Here and now. But he fancied her.

So? He'd fancied women before.

Not women he could easily picture being a mother. He had the girls to think of. They wouldn't be able to bear another loss if this didn't work out. And there were Rebecca's broken dreams to consider.

'Come to Bali. Find some balance. Make peace with yourself.'

His sister's words rang in his ears. The old him hadn't had time for all that hippy nonsense. But he had to be a parent. Now. And figure out what the hell to do with this clinic. Also now.

So, no. He wouldn't be hiring Rebecca.

He opened his mouth to say as much, but instead something different came out. 'We're an international charity so we can avoid some of the visa hurdles. It does mean that the work you'd do would be largely voluntary. We could offer housing, food and a small stipend in exchange for consultancy—' He saw her eyes grow wider and wider as he continued. He pulled a quick U-turn. 'But the fact you're staying in a resort strongly suggests you're here on holiday. Not job-hunting. So it's all irrelevant, right?'

She scrunched up her nose. 'True…'

She drew out the vowels until they faded away, in a manner that filled him with a stupid helium hit of hope.

'Is there a "but" in there?'

'Let's just say I haven't been going to the juice bar across the street from the clinic solely because of the beverages.'

He frowned. 'Are you sick? Do you need medical care?'

'No.' She waved away his concern. 'I—' She

took in a deep breath, then put on a brave smile. 'This trip is me regrouping. I have a pretty big savings account, courtesy of the GP surgery I'm no longer opening. I thought I'd surf a bit and then go home, but I think I'm still…you know…' She pinched her fingers together into a yoga relaxation position. 'Finding myself? Or finding a new self?' She held her hands up in a *Who knows?* gesture.

'Any progress on that front?'

She lifted her shoulders up to her ears. 'Not sure. At this point I don't even know if I want to find the old me.'

'I hear you,' Noah said emphatically. 'I don't know if the old me can do what the new me needs to do.'

'Sounds like we both have some decisions to make.'

He nodded.

The waitress approached and they both ordered. Neither of them chose the satay. For some reason it made them both giggle.

Since when did he *giggle*?

When the waitress had left he asked, 'What made you come here? To Bali?'

She took a sip of her drink—ginger and lemongrass iced tea—gave a self-deprecating laugh, then answered his question. 'I came to Bali be-

cause I found an all-women's surf and yoga resort, promising to help me find my Zen.'

'And have you?' He was surprised to realise
he really wanted to know. Was it even possible?
To find this unachievable 'Zen'?

'Well, I'm not wallowing under my childhood
duvet at my grandmother's house any more, but
I wouldn't say I'm the most serene person on
earth. I still love a good spreadsheet!' The smile
wilted. 'Spreadsheets were an issue in my last
relationship.'

'What's wrong with spreadsheets?'

'I know!' She laughed again. 'My ex said they
hemmed him in. He obviously did not understand that spreadsheets create order and order
means progress.'

'That's a big yes in my book.'

Her smile was a flash of sunshine.

He doubled back to something she'd glossed
over. 'Were you raised by your grandmother?'

She nodded. 'Nanny Bea. She stepped in
when my parents died.'

'Oh, I'm sorry.' Losing parents was terrain he
didn't enjoy revisiting.

*Well, done, Noah. You're batting a thousand
here.*

Rebecca waved off his apology. 'Don't be. I
mean, it would've been great to have had my par-

ents, but I haven't ever really known differently. Besides, who can fight the ocean and win?'

'Sorry. I'm not following.'

'My dad and my granddad were fishermen,' she explained. 'My mum went out with them one day because she said she never saw them enough and…' Her voice grew hollow as she continued. 'There was a big storm. No one came back.'

'And yet you surf?'

She gave a sad smile. 'What is it they say? Know thine enemy?' She cleared her throat and brightened her smile. 'I don't surf the crazy big waves. Just enough to know my limits. Anyway, I can't really remember them it was so long ago. Just snippets. I've always tried to focus on what I *do* have rather than what I don't.'

The comment lodged in his heart, and again he raised his glass to hers.

'Not that I've been a shining example of that ethos lately,' she said. 'To be honest, these past few months I've made an art of focusing on everything my ex has that I don't. A spouse. A child. A house with a garden and a job he—' Abruptly she stopped herself. 'I'm sorry. I think I've got verbal diarrhoea. Or someone gave me truth serum.' She held up her glass and gave it an accusing look. 'What do they put in this tea? Sorry, I'm really oversharing. Ding-ding!' She rang an imaginary bell. 'Taxi for one!'

'No.' He put his hand on hers. 'Stay. I like it.'

It was better than listening to his own thoughts. To the self-admonishments running on a loop in his head. *Woulda, shoulda, coulda...* So many things he would've done differently if only he'd seen what was coming.

She gave a low whistle. 'Wow. You're like— You're a rare mythical creature.'

Their eyes met, and once again he felt an electric current pass between them.

Suddenly she schooched forward, perched on the edge of her seat and, eyes glistening said, 'I've got an idea.'

He leant forward, his arms on the table. 'I'm all ears.'

'You know all this "finding myself" stuff? Letting the universe "gift" me with what I need?'

'Yes...' he answered, not entirely sure where this was going.

'Well, it seems you've got to do some of that, too. And as we both like lists and spreadsheets and plans so much...' She paused, her eyes alight with excitement about whatever it was she was going to propose. 'What if we let the universe call it with a coin toss? You know—whether or not I work here.'

He couldn't hide his shock. 'You'd do that? Stay based on the flip of a coin?'

'Sure. I agreed to give up a job I loved at Nottingham Children's Hospital to move to Cornwall for a man who turned out to be a weasel, so why not let a coin decide whether or not I stay in Bali and do some voluntary work for a good cause?' She gave his hand a pat. 'And don't worry. You're not the good cause. I'm sure you can do just fine without me.'

He gave her a rueful smile. 'I'm not so sure about that. It'd make my cousin happy.'

She shot him a look. One that he was pretty sure meant he'd stuck his foot in it.

'Go for it,' he said definitively. 'I'd love a list-making, spreadsheet-loving plan-maker on staff.'

Rebecca grinned and picked up her backpack. She dug around for a second, then produced a British coin with Queen Elizabeth on one side and what appeared to be a female warrior on the other. He smiled. If Rebecca were on a coin this would be how he'd portray her. Fiery and proud when she needed to be. Vulnerable and open when she'd decided to trust someone.

How had it come so easily to her? Trusting him in the way she had?

She handed the coin to Noah, her eyes bright. 'I'll call it—you flip it. Heads I'm staying. Tails I head back to Blighty the day after tomorrow.'

A sense of urgency gripped him. He couldn't let this woman go. Not now. Not yet.

He flipped the coin. They watched it twirl up into the air. Heads, then tails. Heads, then tails.

He caught the coin in one hand and flipped it onto the back of the other. He lifted his fingers away and held the coin out so they could both see.

Rebecca blinked her surprise.

Noah wondered if he should start leaving everything up to the flip of a coin. He met Rebecca's gaze head-on and said, 'Well, would you take a look at that…?'

CHAPTER FIVE

REBECCA HELD OUT the clipboard for her patient's mum to sign, then knelt down so she was at eye level with Miriam, an adorable little French girl who had quite an impressive sunburn. It wouldn't blister or scar, but judging from the tears that had been shed during the examination it definitely stung.

In her admittedly rusty French, Rebecca said, 'And you're going to be heading right back to your hotel to drink plenty of water in the shade, right? Maybe have a rest?'

The gap-toothed little girl nodded, tears clinging to her dark lashes, then sniffed. 'Will I still get to swim with the dolphins before I go?'

It was all Rebecca could do not to pull the poor little thing into her arms for a consolation hug. But there was the sunburn…and also her mum had said the reason the sunburn had come about was because the little girl had refused to put on the protective top and hat she'd brought with her to keep the sun off her child's delicate skin.

She remembered the advice Noah had given his nieces yesterday afternoon, when they'd run into the clinic and begged to go snorkelling to make up for the session they were meant to have had the other day, when Kylie had her accident. She repeated it now. 'Good things come to those who wait.'

A tiny little shiver slipped down her spine as she remembered how he'd glanced across at her, their eyes clashing as they always did, sparking the thought that he might not just be talking about snorkelling. Then he'd steered the children out to the courtyard as if he said suggestive things to her all the time.

Which, if her first week at the clinic was anything to go by, he didn't.

After their shared moment of insanity—leaving whether or not she stayed in Bali up to a coin toss—practicalities had taken over. Rebecca had seen Kylie off at the airport, packed up her things at the resort and relocated to the clinic. Since then, Noah had only spoken to her when absolutely necessary. Which made all her patient appointments a blessed relief from the tension she felt whenever she was near him.

Whatever had possessed her? Not only to tell

him he was gorgeous and that she fancied the pants off him, but also that he wasn't her type?

She'd clearly been gripped by a moment's insanity. The break-up of her relationship, her dream to open a GP surgery that had never got off the ground and her subsequent wallowing had finally taken their toll.

Mercifully, he'd made sure all the 'settling in' jobs had been doled out to her, which was handy for getting to know everyone. But Rebecca was fairly certain that hadn't been his aim. The aim had been to avoid her.

Now she had two men on two different islands who wanted nothing to do with her. Terrific. At least she hadn't planned her entire future with Noah. She cringed as she remembered showing her ex the retirement plans she'd thought they should start following, so that they'd be able to help their future children onto the housing ladder whilst ensuring that their golden years together would be trouble-free.

Anyway, thank God she genuinely loved the work. It would tide her over until they found someone to replace her.

The job was quite bespoke. So far she'd been using a mix of her GP and paediatric skills. No surgeries yet, but there were some being scheduled. But right now sunburn was the name of the game.

A few teardrops plopped onto Miriam's chubby little-girl cheeks. Her mum moved in.

'Mon cherie. Ne pleure pas, ma petite.'

Don't cry, little one.

The woman carefully drew her daughter to her, swept the tears away with her thumbs and pressed a kiss onto her forehead.

'I wanted to see the dolphins,' the little girl wailed.

An increasingly familiar pinch in her heart caused Rebecca's smile to flicker. Then came the rush of longing. And…yes…there it was… the deep ache in her core.

The Noah Effect.

The man had ridiculously powerful phero-mones. They were practically pleading with Re-becca's reproductive system to stage a coup and make good on the world's need for little baby Noahs.

The mum, clearly misinterpreting Rebecca's maternal pangs, offered an apologetic smile. 'She's been talking about the dolphins ever since we landed, but we had so much pre-booked. You know how it is… You make plans. You feel you should see them through. Anyhow, we thought we'd save the dolphins for last, as a sort of fare-well treat.'

'When do you leave?'

'Demain.'

Tomorrow.

Rebecca nodded and made commiserating noises. Her eyes flicked between the two. The sunburn was bad, but not so bad that it had blistered. There was the chance of a fever setting in—or, if the skin broke, an infection, but...

What was it her grandmother was always saying? *'Life's for living,'* That was the first part. And then, when she knew Rebecca needed reminding that not everything went according to plan, she would add, *'Even if it does hurt sometimes'*.

She sat back on her heels and suggested to Miriam, knowing her mum was tuned in to every word, 'Perhaps if you stay in today, make sure you use the gel, give the anti-inflammatories some time to take effect and always wear a long-sleeved T-shirt with one of those hats that has a neck guard, you could go?' She gave Miriam's arm a light touch. 'You could do that, couldn't you? Wear a hat and a T-shirt if it means swimming with the dolphins?'

Happy tears ran down her cheeks into her wide gap-toothed grin. *'Oui. Absolutement! Oh, Maman, les dauphins!'*

After a few more precautions about what to watch out for, Rebecca waved them off from her examination room door. Her breath caught in her throat when Noah appeared from around the corner. He clearly hadn't been expecting to see her, because for the first time that week when their eyes met his instinct was to smile. And then, as if he'd given himself a lightning-fast telling-off, the smile was pressed into a thin, concentrated frown.

For goodness' sake! She got that he didn't want to be her boyfriend, but it didn't mean he had to scowl every time he saw her. What was the point in her staying if it made him uncomfortable? The man had enough on his plate without feeling he also had to keep her at arm's length.

She decided to put some more of Nanny Bea's advice into play. She pulled a coin out of her pocket. The same one that had landed her here in the clinic.

'Catch.' She threw it before he could dissuade her.

He caught it in one hand and slapped it down on the back of the other. Something lit in his eyes that she hadn't seen since the last time she'd left her fate to the toss of a coin. Engagement. An active interest in what she wanted.

Ooh… This was a bit more like it.

'What are you calling?' he asked, his low voice humming along her spine so it was almost as if he'd stroked it with his hand.

'Heads I stay. Tails I get out of your hair.'

His eyes snapped to hers. 'Why would you leave? Aren't you happy?'

'I like the *work* well enough,' she countered, with a bravura she wasn't entirely sure she felt.

She put a hand on her hip to make herself look more cavalier. His gaze dropped to her hip, then took its time working its way back up to her eyes. Her smile twitched.

'What are you saying?' he demanded. 'The accommodation isn't good enough?'

She pursed her lips. He knew damn straight she wasn't talking about the villa. The clinic, it turned out, had been a luxury resort up until the financial crisis a while back. Noah's father, a property developer, had bought it as an investment and then, after his mum had died, Noah and his sister had been gifted the site, refashioning it into a clinic.

Not that she'd learnt this from Noah. Dr Karja, the doctor she'd met on that first day, had told her. She still had a lot of unanswered questions about the place, but the state of it was not one of them.

No. It was Noah who was the problem.

'I want to help you,' she said.

A divot formed between his brows. 'You *are* helping. You work every day.'

Great. He was going to make her say it. *Okay.*

Fine. 'Yes. I know. But I'm getting the feeling my presence here isn't helping *you.*'

'What? Don't be ridiculous,' he blustered, and then, after a long hard stare at the coin in his hand, he clenched it tight and put it in his pocket. He closed the space between them. 'I've got a lot going on right now.'

'I'm not contesting that,' she countered. 'Losing your sister and brother-in-law as well as gaining two children and a busy health clinic isn't exactly a small blip on the life-change chart.'

His expression barely changed, but she saw something. Something she hadn't noticed before. His pain went deeper than that. Straight to his marrow.

Why are you holding everything that hurts you so close to your heart?

Every pore in her body ached to help him. She'd felt it, too. That need to punish herself when her world had fallen to pieces. The pain had been visceral. Traumatic. As if the memories themselves had morphed into malignant cells, eating away at her ability to see life through anything but a grey, miserable lens. But couldn't he see it wouldn't help?

She readjusted her pose, crossing her arms over her chest, and said, 'Look, I'm all for seeing what the universe throws in my lap, but not if it comes at the expense of your happiness. Be honest. Is my being here adding to your list of problems?'

He continued to stare into her eyes, as if seeking the answer there. 'No.'

'Then why are you avoiding me?'

'I'm not! I—' He stopped himself and put up his hands. 'I am. I have been. I—' He gave a self-effacing laugh, lifting his eyes up to the ceiling. 'My sister would have a field-day with this.'

Rebecca leant against the wall, indicating that she was prepared to listen.

'Did Mel tell you what she and my sister nicknamed me after med school?'

This should be interesting. She was pretty sure it wasn't Mr Guava, Lime and Pineapple Crush.

'The Ostrich,' he said.

'What? Why?'

'They claimed that whenever anything happened that hadn't been added to my diary months in advance, I stuck my head in the sand.'

'You're a doctor. A *surgeon*. You have to act spontaneously all the time!'

He held his hands out. 'That's what *I* said!'

They stared at one another for a moment, then laughed. How was it that they leapt to one another's defence so easily?

Because somehow you already know *each other.*

His laugh died away and then, self-effacingly he added, 'I did the same thing with relationships.'

She nodded, bracing herself for news of a girlfriend waiting back in Sydney.

'I had a relationship. A long one.'

'And…?'

'And she wanted to get married, and I never asked.'

A lightbulb popped on. 'And you're regretting it now?'

He shook his head. 'No. Maybe… I mean, having some help with the girls would be good, but—' He shook his head again and said more solidly, 'No. The point I'm trying to make is that I didn't ever really have what you'd call a steady girlfriend after that.'

She thought for a moment, then asked Noah a question she'd had to ask herself. 'Do you push everything in your life to the side for medicine? Use it as an excuse for not dealing with the other aspects of your life?'

'Wow.' Noah stuffed his hands in his pockets and took a step back. 'I feel seen.'

'You have to know it to call it,' she said gently.

He leant against the wall, mirroring her pose. 'I don't trust myself right now. You know…' He pointed with one of his fingers between the two of them.

She frowned. Was he trying to say he liked her, too?

Before the thought could find purchase, he continued, 'I don't know how to juggle it all. I feel like I'm failing the girls already. I don't know what to do and I've only just begun.'

The confession bashed into her like a wrecking ball. He might as well have reached into his chest, handed her his heart and said, *Here. Do what you can with it. I don't know how it works any more.*

She almost laughed.

'Who does?' she parried. 'It isn't like any parent knows how to do it beforehand. There aren't manuals for what you're going through. No instructional videos you can watch to figure it out—' She stopped herself. 'Well, there are...' She rattled off a few romcoms she'd binge-watched during the darker days of her post-break-up despair. 'They're fictional, of course, but do you know what they all have in common?'

'Tell me,' he said, and his body language was practically screaming, *I'll take any advice right now, so long as it helps.*

'For a while, everything goes unbelievably wrong.' Especially with the romance.

'Wow.' He pulled a face. 'Thanks for the pep talk.'

'No, listen. That's not the endgame. Yes, there's chaos—but you know what else almost always happens?'

'Go on, then, Miss The Universe Already Knows My Fate.'

She smiled, pleased he wasn't turning on his heels and stomping away. 'The hero realises he can't do it all alone.'

'You mean he can't go all ostrich and hope when he pulls his head out of the sand everything will be okay again?'

This was good. He was still able to poke fun at himself.

''Fraid not. Not in your case, anyway.' She pressed her hands to her heart. 'I know I've kind of pushed my way into your life—'

He held up a hand. 'No, you didn't. The universe guided you to me.'

She searched his voice and his face for hints of sarcasm, and was surprised to be met with a warm, grateful smile. 'Well,' she began, not wanting to overstep the mark, 'as it has guided me here, I'm sure it's for more reasons than my medical skills. So if it doesn't stress you out… if there is any way I can help share your load, I will do it. I'm a great babysitter. I can do arts

and crafts. Finger-painting is one of my spe-
cialties.'

*Why are you doing a testimonial on your skills
with children? You're a paediatrician.*

But she couldn't stop herself. This was definitely her reproductive system staging that coup.

To her shock, it seemed to be working.

The more she spoke, the more it seemed her
words were physically entering him. Chipping
away at whatever was holding him together. He
parted his lips, as if to say something that had
been dredged up from the depths of his soul—
and then the Tannoy sounded.

An urgent call to the emergency entrance.

The shutters fell over his eyes. Work Noah
was back.

He turned to go, glancing at his watch as he
did so. Abruptly he froze, his face twisted in
pain.

'What?'

'I'm supposed to meet the girls at five at the
villa.'

'I'll do it,' she offered reflexively.

His eyes snapped to hers and held them. 'No.
I'll see if I can find someone—'

'Noah,' she cut in. 'This isn't me trying to be
the next girlfriend you'll have to ghost.'

Okay, that was a tiny white lie. She really

wouldn't be sad if she was his girlfriend and he snogged her, but she genuinely did want to help.

'You've helped me by giving me work. Reminding me of my purpose.' As the words came out, she realised how true they were. Her voice caught in her throat. 'Let me return the favour. It's nothing more than that.'

He opened his mouth, presumably to protest, but nothing came out.

She opened her palms to show she was feeling as vulnerable as he was. 'Even ostriches need to ask for help.'

The Tannoy sounded again.

They stared at one another. It was decision time.

He bowed his head in acknowledgement. 'Thank you.'

He gave her directions to his place, which lay at the far end of the property, and said he'd text the girls' babysitter to let her know Rebecca would be coming.

'Thank you,' he said again, turning to head back to the clinic.

'Not a problem. Hey!' She called after him. 'What did it say? The coin?'

He blinked deliberately, as if debating whether or not to tell her. 'Stay.'

When he'd gone, Rebecca had the strangest

feeling that he hadn't been telling her what was on the coin at all, but what was in his heart.

'And then what?' Ruby asked, her eyes glistening with delight.

And Isla cried, 'Tell us!'

'And then he asked if I'd had a facelift!'

Ruby and Isla frowned in confusion, until Rebecca put her hands on her cheeks and drew them back, so she looked as if she was caught in a wind tunnel. The girls fell about laughing, as if she'd just told them the funniest thing in the world.

'What's everyone laughing about?'

Rebecca's spine instantly turned buttery as Noah's rich Australian drawl poured warmth through her. When their eyes met, she felt as though a bottle of champagne had opened up inside her.

'Everything all right?'

She nodded, to stop herself from giggling coquettishly.

How had she gone from thirty-seven to seventeen in a millisecond?

No mystery there.

Noah wanted her to stay. And she liked it.

Since they'd last seen one another she'd elbowed a raft of insecurities to one side to make room for something far more pleasurable. A crush.

A practical one, of course. There were very strict 'look but don't touch' rules. 'Enjoy but don't get attached.' It actually made sense to allow herself the butterflies that took flight every time she saw him. Seeing him should be a joy—not torture. And as she'd be leaving Bali in a few months a secret crush wouldn't hurt anyone.

She stood back as the girls flew across the small patio area towards him.

His smile became unchecked. This version of him was more open. Less taut and prepared for attack, and more guardian warrior prepared to protect. Her crush doubled in size. Who wouldn't be smitten by a man prepared to take on the world for his sister's children?

Isla threw her arms around his waist. 'Paman!' she cooed

And her sister followed suit with her own impassioned, 'You came back!'

Their depth of emotion made tears prick at the back of Rebecca's throat. It was the same love she felt for her grandmother.

With the loss of their parents, and their worlds sent topsy-turvy, these girls didn't only love him—they needed him. He was their rock. And he was doing everything in his power to be strong for them, no matter how new it was to him. No wonder he didn't have time for a girlfriend. She didn't think she'd have the brain power to absorb becoming an instant parent as well as someone's partner.

But that was the thing, wasn't it? Brains didn't fall in love. Hearts did.

Noah picked one girl up with each arm and twirled them round, to their absolute delight.

Her heart melted.

This, she thought. *This is what I wanted when I dreamt of having a family.*

She squinted up at the sky, wondering if the universe was reminding her that families didn't always come via the traditional path. Love, marriage, baby carriage.

Families could come shaped like this. Or, in fact, like her own tiny family of two.

Perhaps her childhood dream of having what society deemed traditional had overridden her gut instinct that her ex might not be The One.

They'd had shared interests. Similar jobs. They'd found one another attractive enough.

She'd been so *sensible* about it all.

Maybe that had been the problem.

She pressed her hands to her heart as the girls begged Noah to twirl them round again—which, of course, he did, making it crystal-clear that he needed them every bit as much as they needed him. How could he not? They were proof his sister and brother-in-law had existed. Prescient reminders that the simple things—like a loved one returning home from work—were what really made a relationship strong. That sort of thing couldn't be put on a spreadsheet.

Flashes of just how wrong she and her ex had got it crackled painfully through her. Their lives had been so busy with work they'd had only snatched moments together, careers taking precedence over everything else to the point where their actual romance hadn't been much more than a highlights reel. None of the depth and glue of real-life events that held couples together.

And then she'd issued an ultimatum. *Marry me and let's build our lives together or let's break up.*

She winced. Hadn't Noah's girlfriend done the same thing to him? *Ouch.*

Only her boyfriend *had* proposed. They'd drawn up practical plans, retrained as GPs, all the while scraping together whatever money they could to buy a practice in Cornwall and be near her grandmother. It had all been going perfectly to plan—right up until it had all fallen apart.

Although honestly… A niggle had lodged in her chest the moment David had slid that ring on her finger. One that had scratched and pushed against her conscience, virtually begging her to acknowledge the fact that they weren't following their hearts. That this wasn't how love worked. Structuring their lives—effectively cornering one another—into a lifestyle that wouldn't allow them to grow.

That niggle, of course, had turned out to be foresight, but heigh-ho. She gave her shoulders a shake and popped her eyes open. It wasn't always fun to be right.

'Paman!' Isla tugged on Noah's hand. 'We're hungry!'

'Are you?' He crouched into a wild animal pose. 'As hungry as a bear?'

He roared. They screamed and squealed. Isla literally jumped into his arms, begging him never to do that again, whilst Ruby jumped up and down shouting, 'Again! Again! I'm a hungry bear!'

He roared and chased them round the patio until they all collapsed in a heap on the small arc of grass that outlined a beautiful koi pond, the three of them giggling and catching their breath.

Watching Noah with the girls, stepping outside his comfort zone—or perhaps stepping into it?—felt like witnessing living proof that you couldn't *organise* someone into loving you. No matter how good the spreadsheet. It had to happen naturally.

A sharp stab of loneliness pierced her heart as she watched them disentangle themselves from one another. It was something she'd never experienced. Or she didn't remember anyway. A rough and tumble with her parents. It was something she'd ached for. The big, boisterous, love-infused silliness that only family members could share.

She caught herself with a terse reminder that these girls weren't with their parents either. They were resilient. Just as she had been. And with this version of Noah they'd flourish.

As if sensing her gaze on them, Noah looked up, instinctively wrapping his arms round each of the girls' shoulders.

'Thanks for looking after them. I wouldn't have accepted your offer, but—'

She stopped him there, before the tears pricking at the back of her eyes came. 'You can't help it if an urgent call comes in when you're meant to leave.' She was going to leave it there, but then, remembering their earlier conversation, forced herself to maintain eye contact and said, 'You can always ask me. Any time. I want to help.'

Something passed between them. Something understood.

The feeling was so intense she smiled and took a step forward, half expecting Noah to open up his arms and pull her in to join them, before remembering that, even though he'd peeled off one layer of himself, he hadn't exactly split himself in half and revealed all. He hadn't said he wanted to be friends. He definitely hadn't said he wanted to be lovers.

Wait! What?

And just like that she was mentally disrobing him.

Stay.

The word circled round her chest like warm honey. A sensation far too sexy for anyone's good.

She was about to make her apologies and leave, see what sort of takeout meal she could find on the high street, when Noah cleared his throat and said, 'We were going to have an Aussie dinner night.'

Ruby cheered and Isla started marching around, saying, 'Shrimp on the barbie! Shrimp on the barbie!'

Noah rubbed his jaw and said, 'It won't be much more than that, but you're welcome to stay.'

Rebecca hesitated.

Stay.

To work? To play? Both?

She didn't have what Kylie did. The ability to live in the moment, enjoy her body and the men who wanted to pleasure it, only to move on to the next one when that didn't pan out.

She wanted love. Not lust. No matter how many intense looks they shared, the truth was Noah wasn't in any place to offer her anything more than a plate full of grilled shrimp and a few months' voluntary work.

'Life's for living, my little cupcake!' Her grandmother's voice rang in her ear. *'Find the zest!'*

But what if 'the zest' was tall, dark, grieving his sister, and trying to figure out how to balance work and raising two little girls?

Before she could pull some sort of excuse out of the ether, Ruby and Isla each grabbed one of her hands and guided her round the villa to a back patio she hadn't seen yet. She gasped. It was so beautiful. The whole area was strung with fairy lights, creating a magical feeling. And the thick stone slabs of the patio extended to a huge, modern, open-air kitchen.

Beneath soaring arched beams there was a gorgeous teak table, a massive kitchen island made out of a huge tree round, and everything a cooking obsessive could ever want hanging from the wooden dowels strategically placed along the immaculate countertops. A wooden staircase ran the length of the back wall up to a thatch-and-beam-covered room where, beneath a broad ceiling fan, she could glimpse invitingly deep sofas and low bookshelves stuffed to bursting. It was her kind of room.

'Don't get too excited,' Noah cautioned when he saw her gaze return to the kitchen. 'My sister's husband was the chef. Not me. They had this wonderland added on to the villa when they moved in to run the clinic. I cook bachelor food, caveman style, and other than that I can pour a mean bowl of cereal.'

As her lips twitched into a smile at the warning, a woman dressed in the clinic's restaurant uniform came through a discreet bamboo gate at the edge of the patio and set a tray of clingfilm-covered plates on a table next to the barbecue.

They all gathered round.

Shrimp. Chicken. Vegetables. All threaded onto tidy skewers. There were little bowls filled with dips. Satay. Chilli oil. And a few other things she recognised but couldn't name.

'Australian, you say?' She grinned across at Noah, who rubbed his jaw again, this time in embarrassment.

'Well, Australia's pretty multicultural. Myself included.' He gave her a sheepish smile. 'I'm not much of a cook, but if my Aussie father taught me one thing, it was how to grill meat.'

The fact he'd mentioned his father felt significant. There'd been no mention of him before. Perhaps Noah was unpeeling more layers of himself than she'd thought. Testing the waters to see how much he could trust her with his carefully protected private life.

'Well, in that case I'd be grateful to accept your invitation,' she said with a small curtsey.

'Good.' He spread his hand across his chest in a show of gratitude. *'Good.'*

CHAPTER SIX

'Are you sure?' Noah shook his head. 'You don't have to.'

'Absolutely.' Rebecca held out her palm and flicked her fingers in a *Hand it over* gesture. 'You made dinner—the least I can do is dry the dishes you are so gallantly washing.'

Noah gave her a bemused side-eye. 'It's not really gallant when there isn't anyone else to do it, is there?'

'My—' she began, and then rephrased the sentence. 'I know people who would rely on the restaurant staff to do them.'

Noah said nothing, but wondered if 'people' meant her ex. Even the veiled mention of him made his skin itch with distaste. Cheating was bad enough. But this guy sounded as if he'd set up a whole other family before informing Rebecca. No wonder she didn't want to go back to the UK.

He had to admit he had a bit of the same feeling about going back to Oz. Sydney was technically home, but his happiest memories were actually here in Bali. They'd only come once a year as children, during the long school holidays, but his dad had never come and along with his mum and his sister, Bali had always managed to feel more like home than Sydney ever had.

The houses they'd lived in growing up had always been more of an advertisement for his father's success than a home. Bigger, showier, with less and less freedom to play, for fear of messing something up or breaking something. The fact that he'd moved into a condominium that pretty much said the same thing—*I'm so good at my job I live in a house that looks like it should be in a magazine spread*—was suddenly discomfiting.

Had he spent his career trying to prove to his dad he was good enough, despite his decision not to follow him into the family business?

'Come on.' Rebecca grinned at him, hand still extended. 'Many hands make light work.'

He gave her a fresh tea towel and turned the taps on full-blast to fill up the sink. 'I really should be getting the girls to help,' he said. 'My sister and I were always on drying duty with my mum, but—'

He closed his eyes, not knowing if he was trying to stop the memories or summon them.

Him and his sister, standing on step stools as
their mum handed them dishes and cutlery,
while their dad kicked back in the sound-proof
home cinema, watching whatever sport was on
that night. For a man who purported to adore
women, he had never respected them very much.
Especially not their mother.

Noah started when Rebecca reached over to
turn the hot tap off.

'I hope you're going to wear those.' Rebecca
nodded to the pink washing up gloves hanging
on a wooden rod to the left of the large butler's
sink.

He snorted and then, considering the steam
rising from the froth of bubbles, reconsidered.
Putting on a comedic suave voice he intoned,
'I'm comfortable enough with my masculinity
to wear pastels.'

Her smile widened as she watched him put on
the pink washing up gloves. 'Would that extend
to changing out of your dour black scrubs into
adorable pink paediatric scrubs?'

His answer was swift. 'No.'

'Okay…' She looked away, stung.

'Sorry. I didn't mean to snap, I—'

He had a choice here. Clam up like he usually
did. Pound his emotions into submission. Push
her away. Or take the path he normally didn't,

as he had this afternoon when he'd found himself admitting he was in over his head.

'The black scrubs…they're not "mourning scrubs"…'

'I shouldn't have asked. It's not my business,' Rebecca began fastidiously drying a plate and placing it on the bamboo stand beside the sink. She held out her hand. 'Next dish, please. I've got an early start tomorrow, so I should push off soon.'

He swore to himself. *Nice one, Noah. Hurt the woman who's doing her best to help.*

It was a pointed reminder that his universe wasn't the only one. She'd been hurt, too. Had the rug pulled straight out from under her. Sure, in a totally different way from him, but they were both grieving for futures they'd never have.

Which made him stop in his tracks. What sort of future had he been planning for, exactly? One where he told himself he was a good man because he sent money from a job he loved to a sister he loved but never visited, just in case she asked him what the hell he was doing with his life?

That was definitely the track he'd been on.

Why did the idea of having a family of his own scare him so much?

Because caring meant loss. Or betrayal.

Loss of his mother. Betrayal from his father.

He hadn't grown up in the ideal family. Hadn't been set good examples. How the hell was he supposed to know how to get any of it right?

His sister hadn't let that scare her.

He turned off the cold tap and faced Rebecca. 'I'm sorry. I— My fallback position is defensiveness. To shut things down. It's not a good trait.'

'It's fine. You're stressed, and I'm pushing buttons I don't know about. Plate, please.' Her voice was bright. Too chirpy to be genuine.

Fix it, Noah.

How? Whenever he'd upset a girlfriend before he'd usually just called an end to it. Told her things were getting too complicated.

Ostrich!

Rebecca wasn't his girlfriend! She was his… Colleague didn't seem right, even though it was accurate. She was… He heard his sister's voice: *She's your sign from the universe.*

He began scrubbing the plates, turning over options as to how to get the conversation started again.

Sorry, I'm such an asshole.

Nope.

Pink scrubs don't really match my complexion.

Double no.

Do you know this is the longest amount of time I've spent in Bali since my mum passed away?

Closer…

I'm not sure I want to go home, but I don't know if staying is an option.

He had the girls to think of. At this very moment his cousin was back in Sydney, drawing up a list of candidates for the position of full-time nanny. He'd be able to lean on Mel for a bit of support there. Though he had his doubts. Chances were his father would be more likely to want to see the girls in Sydney than here. And here he had the clinic. And the girls had their friends. And his brother-in-law's family were only a short flight away.

After a few moments Rebecca said, 'I become useful when I'm stressed. Too useful. I make charts and lists and offer solutions to problems that people may not want fixing. Or, if they do, they probably need to fix them themselves. I also talk too much.'

She shot him a shy, apologetic smile, then grabbed a handful of spoons and began to dry them fastidiously.

This had gone from bad to worse.

He turned to her. 'I wear black scrubs because they make me feel like a ninja.'

She snorted and rolled her eyes. 'Yeah, right.'

'Seriously.'

She threw him a *Try again, pal* look.

Screw it. He was going to walk right out to the end of the plank on this one.

'I know it sounds completely ridiculous, but as a kid, when I first started thinking of becoming a doctor, I used to think if I became a superhero doctor I'd be the Samurai Surgeon.'

Her lips began to twitch. 'You did what?'

He couldn't believe he was actually admitting this. It was a childhood dream that could have died with his sister if he'd let it, but something about Rebecca made him want her to know him. The *real* him.

He relaxed into the storytelling. 'It's completely true. I used to want to do martial arts as a kid, like my Indonesian uncles.'

He sliced the air between them in a couple of moves that might've looked cool if he hadn't been wearing pink washing up gloves.

'I am deeply jealous of your ninja skills,' Rebecca grinned. 'Come on, then. Show us some more moves.'

The playful mood drained out of him. He pulled the washing up gloves off and hung them on the rack. 'My dad pushed me into playing footie, rugby, Aussie rules... You know—tough guy sports.' He lowered his voice to mimic his father's. "'What the use of being built like you are if you're not going to put it to good use?'"

Rebecca frowned. 'He's seen *Crouching Tiger, Hidden Dragon*, hasn't he? Or *Karate Kid*? Please tell me he's seen *Karate Kid*.'

'Right?' Noah held his hands out, gratified that someone else understood his childhood dream.

He was going to leave it at that, but decided, *What the hell? In for a penny and all that.*

'I think it'd be fair to say my father was never one to bend like the willow.' He hoped the phrase translated. It was a sort of catch-all for many Eastern philosophical doctrines that recommended going with the flow rather than fighting the inevitable.

Rebeca frowned. 'But isn't your mum—?'

'Indonesian. Yes.' He cleared his throat and added. 'She was. She died seven years back.'

Rebecca's hands flew to cover her mouth as he explained about the illness that had taken her. Bone cancer, of all things. And he'd been completely powerless to stop it.

'I'm so sorry, Noah. I...' She took a step back, as if needing to give this new information some room to settle, then met his eyes straight on. 'For what it's worth I think you look kick-ass in those scrubs. They make you look...erm...' She waved her hand up and down at him, as if it would help the word come to her, before settling on, 'Good.'

The flush sweeping across her cheeks made him fairly certain she'd been thinking of a different word.

He made another chopping move with his hand, to cover up the fact that he liked it that she thought he looked kick-ass in his scrubs. Or maybe he was showing off.

Struth. He hadn't shown off for a girl in he didn't know in how long. School, maybe?

Rebecca gave the space between them a bit of a kick, and somehow they ended up doing a slow motion martial arts fight, culminating in a massive case of the giggles.

Was this what honesty did? Evoke joy?

Rather than feeling exposed, stupid, and desperately wishing he'd kept his mouth shut, he was laughing and enjoying being in his own skin.

They stopped, both panting a bit, and as their laughter died away it morphed into something else. Something…sexier. Heated.

The feelings tore at his heart. Old Noah would've asked if she fancied a bit of 'adult time', but this Noah couldn't. He had responsibilities beyond his work life now. And, just as importantly, he respected Rebecca too much to start something he knew he couldn't finish.

She must've seen the shift in his eyes, because the smile fell from her face. 'Well, I'd better get going.'

He tried to speak, but everything he wanted to say jammed in his throat.

What was it about her that made him want to reach into his chest, pull out his ragged heart and say, *Here. This is what's left of it. Atrophied in parts. Shredded in others. But the core is still beating. Improving, even. And part of the reason it's healing is because of you.*

Who even said stuff like that? TV characters, maybe. But this was real life.

'Fair enough.' He took the tea towel she handed back to him, too aware of the moment when they each had hold of one end.

Rebecca stared at him for a moment, and then, as if she needed to physically break away from the magnetic energy that kept tugging them together, abruptly pulled her huge swathe of hair back and, releasing an elastic band from her wrist, piled it up into a messy knot on top of her head. Loose tendrils of flame-coloured hair shifted round the curves of her face like firelight.

'What?' Rebecca asked, misreading the intensity of his gaze. She started dabbing at her face. 'Do I have food on my face? Bubbles from the washing up?'

He shook his head. She was perfect. 'You're hygienic.'

Nice, Noah. Just what every girl wants to hear. That she's hygienic.

Rebecca dipped her head and to his surprise gave him a shy smile. 'Thanks for letting me join you. It was nice having a family-style meal.'

The words landed in his chest like an arrow with a bittersweet sting.

It was a life he'd never imagined for himself, and quite clearly a life Rebecca had long dreamt of. Kids. A family. Chances were it might have been more painful than pleasurable for Rebecca to spend time with him and the girls. A visual visceral taunt. *Here's what you aren't getting!*

Now that it was over, he had to admit it *had* been really nice to play happy families. Natural, even. Probably the first night together when he and the girls had been this relaxed. Everyone had pitched in with the cooking, the girls donning aprons and white chef's toques they'd unearthed from somewhere. Rebecca had used some of the hairbands from the collection on her wrist to secure thick oven gloves onto the girls' small hands after they'd insisted on turning the barbecuing meat, and then used the same oven gloves as puppets, reducing the girls to streams of laughter as they tried to teach her how to count to ten in Balinese.

Conversation had flowed easily. In fact, making chit-chat with the girls had been much easier with Rebecca there. She didn't do the thing his cousin did—talk to him as if he were a child, too, speaking slowly and clearly about safety and boundaries and bedtimes and structure. He was a bachelor, not an idiot.

Rebecca was different. She spoke to everyone naturally about anything and everything. Enabled the girls to do things helicopter parents like his cousin might not allow. Like turning the meat on a hot barbecue. She turned the safety aspects into fun. It was easy to see why she'd been drawn to paediatrics. She was a natural with children.

And she deserved someone who wanted to give them to her.

At the end of the corridor a huge gale of laughter erupted from the bathroom, where the girls were taking a very splashy-sounding bath. His eyes met Rebecca's.

She flicked her thumb towards the gate that led out into the clinic gardens. 'I'll just sneak off before they're finished.'

'No, please.' The last thing he wanted her to feel like was a spare part. 'Stay. They'll want to say goodnight.'

In truth, sudden departures didn't go down

well with the girls since their parents had been killed.

He got it. They wanted assurances. At six and eight, they weren't unaware of what was going on, and on the face of it were showing remarkable fortitude. But they had nightmares. Tensed when things didn't go strictly to plan. They were too young and too fragile to be reminded on a regular basis that life didn't come with assurances.

So what made you allow Rebecca to be with them this afternoon when you could've sent her to the emergency room in your place?

He knew the answer.

But he couldn't be an ostrich any more. It wasn't Rebecca's job to take care of the children. It was his.

A pitter-patter of feet sounded in the corridor and the girls appeared in their cotton pyjamas, faces scrubbed clean. 'Is she still here?'

Their eyes gleamed when they saw her. They ran over and hugged her round the waist.

Rebecca knelt down to their level. 'I couldn't leave without saying goodbye to you two flower-faces, could I?' She shot a quick look at Noah. 'I'm afraid I've got to go now, but I'll see you again soon, yeah?'

The girls made matching sad noises.

Ruby looked up at Noah, her expression one

of complete innocence. 'Is Rebecca your girl-friend?'

A flush swept up Rebecca's neck to her cheeks.

Noah rubbed the back of his neck. 'No, honey. We work together.'

'But…' Isla began. 'Mummy and Daddy worked together, and they were married.'

'True, but—'

'I should definitely be hitting the road.' Rebecca grabbed her backpack from one of the kitchen chairs and was halfway across the patio before Noah could protest. 'Goodnight, girls. See you tomorrow, okay?'

She didn't bother saying goodbye to him.

After a chorus of goodnights had followed her down the low-lit path, the girls tugged Noah to the sofa for their night-time story ritual.

All of them were clearly feeling Rebecca's absence, because their newly established routine—supper, bath, then sofa time with a story—was considerably more subdued.

'What will it be tonight, then, girls? A fairy tale? Or one of the books your auntie brought over from Australia?'

The girls listlessly pawed through the pile of books he showed them.

Then Ruby pushed them down onto his lap and said, 'Uncle Noah?'

'Yes, poppet?'

'Would you make Rebecca your girlfriend?'

He faltered, trying to come up with some sort of answer. He chose a question instead. 'We're doing all right, aren't we? Us three?'

'Yeah, but...' Isla traced her finger along one of the tattoos on his arm. A dragon. 'It'd be nice if there was someone here who was like a mummy, the same way you're sort of like an *ayah*.'

The Indonesian word for father barely made it out of her mouth before tears began to trickle down her cheeks.

Oh, hell. If Isla was crying that meant— Yup. Ruby was crying, too.

He pulled the girls in close, dropping kisses atop each of their heads. He hadn't even bothered trying to soothe them with words when he'd first flown over, and the tradition, if you could call it that, had stuck. Hugs and kisses had become his language for the times when words would never do. It was what his own mother had done. His father had placated and charmed with words, and they had all been lies in the end.

The girls burrowed into his chest as if they were kittens, each seeking a snuggly purchase as they wept into his shirt. He looked out into the darkness, wishing like hell that Rebecca had stayed.

CHAPTER SEVEN

REBECCA'S SMILE CAME unbidden as Noah appeared at the charge nurse's desk. And then, embarrassingly, a blush. Why did she always turn the colour of a beet when she was near him? She wasn't a twelve-year-old girl any more.

She gave herself a little shoulder-shake, as if that would remind her of the facts here. She was a grown woman trying to put her past behind her with a very interesting job. A job she should be focussing on instead of staring at Noah's hands and wondering what it would feel like if he ran just one of those beautiful surgeon's fingers along her collarbone and—

'Good morning, Dr Stone.'

Ah. So she was Dr Stone again. No more Rebecca. Okay. Cool. She could roll with that. She gave him what she hoped was an officious-looking nod.

He gave her an inquisitive look. 'You're up bright and early.'

Her smile remained fixed as her flush deepened. 'Certainly am!'

That was what happened when sleeping involved having erotic dreams about your new boss. You woke up early and had lots and lots of energy to expend.

Which was fairly different from how she'd used to be. Clinging to every ounce of sleep she could schedule.

Noah reached across the counter, his arm accidentally brushing hers as she reached for a notepad. Her eyes snapped to his as a rippling of goosebumps skittered up her arm.

His gaze quickly dropped away, and she wondered if he'd been imagining her naked, too.

Oh, Lordy.

She began to scribble on the pad as if writing a prescription. *You have a raging case of I-fancy-the-pants-off-you.*

'That's it,' she murmured as her hand started involuntarily drawing little love hearts.

'Rebecca?' Noah's expression turned into a concerned frown and he moved closer to the desk, as if to try and read what she was writing. 'Is everything all right? Do you need help with a patient?'

'Nope. Grand. Everything's lovely.' She crumpled up the paper and stuffed it into her pocket. 'Tickety-boo, in fact. Thank you for enquiring,

Dr Cameron. Just off for a spot of tea in the staffroom. If you'll excuse me?' The Britishisms fell out of her mouth and she barely stopped herself from offering him a curtsey.

Looking at him only made her heart-rate spike, so she did what any mature woman hoping to make a positive impression would—picked up a nearby pamphlet on a monkey sanctuary and tapped it, as if it explained her very odd behaviour, then high-tailed it to the staffroom.

'Thanks for another great day.' The charge nurse, a friendly local woman called Jhoti, took Rebecca's tablet from her and waved it as if it was a trophy. 'You don't know how much it means to us to have you here.'

Rebecca stopped in her tracks. 'I thought you had loads of doctors right now?'

The nurse smiled, then leant in and spoke in a whisper. 'There are a few surgeons around...' Her smile faded away. 'Sort of, anyway.'

'What does that mean?' Rebecca asked. 'Sort of?'

'Well...' The nurse drew out the word, her eyes flicking down the corridor. 'With everything in flux...you know... Dr Cameron hasn't exactly made it clear whether or not the clinic's going to stay open. So we've got some surgeons on holiday here in Bali who've volunteered to do the odd surgery, but no one like you who has committed to working for a few months. He can't shut it down while you're working here.'

Rebecca blinked in surprise. First of all, she was pretty sure she didn't wield that kind of power. Second of all... 'You don't think he'd actually close it, do you?'

The nurse shrugged, then leaned in a bit closer. 'We have no idea. He never really seemed that into it when his sister was running the place. We thought it was for both of them, you know... Given that the place was opened in their mother's memory.'

Rebecca nodded as if she had known, but this was all news to her. It helped a lot of pieces fit into place. Noah's mum had passed away around the time when he'd said he had his last long-term relationship. The two had to be connected. But his not wanting to come here... That wouldn't make sense unless—oh, God—unless he blamed himself for not being able to cure his mother's cancer.

Jhoti looked over her shoulder again. 'It was definitely Indah's passion project. And her husband's. We actually used to call Dr Cameron Dr Cheques and Balances up until the last couple of months, when we discovered how great a doctor he actually is.'

Rebecca knew the comment wasn't mean. It simply spoke to the fact that they didn't know him.

'Maybe if you could let him know how much we love working here…'

'Me?' Rebecca pulled back.

'Yes.' Jhoti gave Rebecca a look, suggesting she was missing something obvious. 'He listens to you. When he talks to us he's always a bit re-moved, but with you…he really listens.'

Another nurse came up to the counter then, ending the conversation, but Rebecca was reel-ing.

Noah listened to her?

It was a fairly big headline, considering she barely had the skills to chat with him without her face turning tomato-red.

But the reality of how big a decision Noah had to make made her concerns about whether or not he had a crush on her pale in compari-son. All of this—the clinic, her volunteer work here and, more to the point, the jobs of the two dozen or so locals who offered invaluable medi-cal aid to the local community—could be shut down in an instant.

Noah could've closed it the day his sister had died, but hadn't. He had a life back in Australia. A high-powered job that had brought him international renown. And the girls' future to think of. Of course he'd go back. It wasn't a question of if. It was a question of when.

The thought twisted her in two.

In such a short time she'd grown to love this place. The cottage hospital feel of the clinic married the two things she loved most about medicine—personalised service and the power to see a medical situation through, no matter the cost.

What if...? What if *she* offered to run it?

The thought gripped her stomach in a way that felt a lot more like excitement than panic. But just as quickly it reversed course.

Was she hoping to fill the gaping void in her life with something that would distract her? Trying to be useful in the way she had been in taking over all the planning for the GP surgery back home? Well, that had ended in epic failure...so perhaps she needed to adopt another tack. Self-preservation.

Rebecca distractedly gave the nurse a wave goodnight, then scuttled out to the garden to call Nanny Bea. Her homing beacon. She might be letting this whole 'taking what the universe presented to her' thing run away with itself.

She tucked herself into a shady nook out in the garden, pulled her phone out of her pocket and dialled the one and only number in 'Favourites'.

After a few moments, she pulled the phone away from her ear and frowned.

Weird.

Her nan always answered the phone at the first ring when she made her daily check-in.

It had rung seven times now.

Rebecca checked her watch. It was ten a.m. back home. She'd always been at home pretty much round the clock when Rebecca had been there.

A shiver of panic swept through her. Maybe something was wrong. What if something had happened to her and no one from the village had checked? Her nan wasn't exactly elderly—she was a vital seventy-seven, and most folk thought she was in her sixties. She regularly won her age category in the local half-marathon, but—

No. This wasn't right. Nanny Bea always answered the phone straight away.

Guilt swept into the cracks of her conscience that anxiety had opened.

What if something had happened to Nanny Bea?

The answering machine clicked in and Rebecca did her best to leave a chirpy message, but she knew it sounded false. She was just about to search for the number for her nan's best friend when she heard footsteps.

'Hey.' Noah stopped in his tracks. His eyes

went to the phone and Rebecca's peculiar expression. 'Everything all right?'

She shook her head. 'I—I don't know.'

CHAPTER EIGHT

Noah's nerve-endings shot to high alert in a way they normally wouldn't for a colleague. 'What's wrong? Is there anything I can do?'

Rebecca shook her head and held up her phone. 'I don't think so. It's my nan. She's not answering the phone.'

'Is that unusual?'

'Yes. But—' Rebecca gave him a pained wince. 'I could be blowing things out of proportion.'

'How do you mean?'

'She could be at the shops. She could be out watering her flowers. She could be—I don't know… Having a life now that her messed-up granddaughter isn't there any more?' She threw up her hands and then let them flop back into her lap, giving an emotive cross between a sigh and fear-laden squeak. 'She's just always there for me, and now she's—she's not.'

Her voice hitched in a way that tugged at Noah's heart. He sat down beside her and took one of her hands in his. 'Do you need to speak to her urgently? Is something wrong?'

Rebecca opened her mouth then quickly pressed her lips together.

'What? You can tell me.'

'I don't think I can.'

'Why?'

'Because it's about you. Well, you and the clinic.' She pulled her hand from his and began to fret at the skin on her thumb.

'What about the clinic? Everything seemed fine when I left.' He threw a look back at the main building and then in the direction of his villa, where he was meant to be meeting the girls.

'No, sorry. I didn't mean—' She tipped her head into her hands. 'Oh, man. I'm really sticking my foot in my mouth. Do you need to go? You look like you have to get home. I'll just— Let's pretend this never happened.'

'Rebecca. What is going on?'

She looked at him then—really looked at him. Her body language shifted, grew stronger, as if she'd made a decision.

'The staff are wondering whether or not you are going to close the clinic down. They're worried for their futures and for some mad reason they think you listen to me. That you trust me.'

She waved her hands. 'I don't know… It's probably all nonsense.'

'No. They're right.' It was empowering, putting words to the mysterious energy that had gripped him since Rebecca had come into his life. 'I do trust you.'

He respected her, too, which was why he was trying to ignore the obvious sexual chemistry they shared. Rebecca deserved better than this version of him.

She pressed her hands to her heart. 'That means a lot to me. Believe me. But…why not them? You've got an amazingly dedicated staff here. Ready and willing to do anything they can to make sure this place stays open.'

He threw another look back at the clinic. 'It isn't that I don't trust them. It's more…' He looked into her beautiful green eyes. 'I don't trust *me*.'

Today it felt doubly true. His cousin was starting to send through the CVs of very well-regarded nannies. Men and women much more qualified than him to raise two little girls. He'd also had a call from his boss back in Sydney, asking when he was thinking about coming back. Noah had said he needed more time, but he could tell there was a limit to his boss's patience. Noah brought in high-profile patients, and without him there they'd need to employ some other big-shot surgeon. One who wasn't juggling all the feelings he'd put on hold for the last couple of decades.

'Why don't you trust yourself?' she asked.

Because I've met you.

It was a mad thought, but it was true. She believed in him in the way his sister had. She saw through all his bravura and...what had she called it?...his broodiness. She saw a kind man. One with a big heart.

He wanted to be that man for the girls and for Rebecca.

Heading back to Sydney meant that man would disappear.

He leant back against the stone wall and threw her a sad smile. 'Have you ever wished you could go back in time and make some changes to the decisions you made?'

She laughed. 'Just about every day of the week! Mostly on the personal front. Being a doctor was always my goal.' Her brow furrowed as she tipped her head to the side to consider him, as if she could see straight into his mind. 'What would you change? You're a successful surgeon. You've got a thriving clinic here—'

'Let me stop you there. The clinic exists because of my sister. I didn't want to have anything to do with it.'

'Why not?'

He held up a hand. 'It isn't caring for the patients that's the problem.' He swept his hand across the gardens. 'It's the packaging.'

Rebecca looked confused. 'Seriously? You have a problem with paradise?'

'I do,' he admitted. 'Because this particular paradise comes with a bunch of conditions.'

She tucked her knees under her chin and gave him an *I'm all ears* look.

It was a story he hadn't told much—if ever. 'My dad isn't what you would call a faithful man.'

Rebecca nodded. She wasn't judging. Just listening. And for that he was grateful. He surprised himself by letting the whole story pour out.

'He's a property developer. Buys beautiful artisan places like this and does them up to high spec for Western tourists.'

'Is that how he met your mother?' Rebecca asked.

He nodded. 'A long time ago, when he didn't have much more than two coins to rub together. He had come here on a surfing holiday with a couple of friends, stayed in a guest house with a ramshackle seafront bar that the owner didn't want to run any more. My mum worked there doing odd jobs. Bartending some days. Cleaning on others.'

He glanced at Rebecca. Not everyone knew he came from such humble roots. Rebecca gave him another encouraging nod, clearly keen for him to continue. So he did. He told her how his dad had convinced the owner to let him run the bar in exchange for a free room. His father had somehow turned the place around and made it one of the most popular tourist nightspots on the island. It had been the beginning of what was to become a massive property empire. One he ran to this day.

'So that's when your parents fell in love?'

He nodded. 'My mum had a really amazing eye for interior decor and helped him design all his places until we were born.' He gave a tight huff of indignation. 'Not that he gave her much credit for either thing. But praise and adulation wasn't something she ever craved, you know? She was just happy knowing we were being looked after and getting amazing educations. Things she hadn't really ever had.'

'Did she have family here?'

He shook his head. 'She was actually an orphan. If she hadn't caught my dad's eye, she might've stayed a cleaner here her whole life.'

'So, that's a good thing, right? That they met? She got to discover some hidden talents. She had you.'

The comment was a pointed one. A reminder

that he wouldn't be here if his parents hadn't got together.

'You say your dad has an eye for the ladies?'

He nodded. 'We weren't really aware of it as kids. He was always off on one business trip or another. Mum always stayed with us. If he needed her for design work he'd send her the briefs or, if it was the school holidays, fly us all out to join him—after he'd had all the lipstick dry cleaned out of his collars, if you get my meaning.'

Rebecca nodded.

He cut to the chase. 'Just as I was fresh out of med school and making my mark in the world of orthopaedics my mum got bone cancer. Stage four.'

She winced.

'All she wanted to do was come back here. Dad had just bought this place for a song after one of the financial crashes, so we thought— why not? If what she really needed was palliative care, my sister and I could sort that out with help from the local hospital, and she could design a last, final tribute to her homeland.'

'So…is that what happened?'

'Nope.' He knew he sounded bitter. 'Dad kept making excuses. Saying he couldn't get a construction team. That it wouldn't be restful for

Mum.' He twirled his finger. 'A ream of excuses, all of which were Class-A bull.'

Rebecca looked alarmed. 'Why would he lie about that?'

'Because he was keeping his latest mistress here.' He nodded towards one of the bungalows that his sister, rather hilariously, had used for putting the rubbish in. 'She'd come to Bali to "get over" a divorce and my dad helped her with that.' He huffed out a disbelieving laugh. 'He kept making excuses as to why Mum couldn't come just yet. One more week this… Next month that… He actually said to me, "As the doctor in the family, it's your job to keep her alive."'

He still didn't begin to know how to forgive his father for that. He was an orthopaedic surgeon, not an oncologist. Not to mention they hadn't even found out about the cancer until it was too late. Not even oncologists were wizards.

'Anyway…' He tugged this hand through his hair. 'Mum died in Australia.'

'Oh, Noah.' Rebecca had tears in her eyes, and her expression was wreathed in compassion when it should've been etched with contempt. 'I'm so sorry.'

He was too. The cancer had been cruel and swift, and even though he couldn't have cured it he was her son. A doctor who should've made her journey more comfortable. And it wasn't as if there hadn't been other places to stay in Bali. He'd just… He'd wanted his dad—just once— to act like a man whose wife, the mother of his children, was the centre of his universe. And he hadn't. Not even knowing she was dying.

Noah knew he'd carry the shame of not standing up to his father to his grave.

In a monotone he explained how, after his mum's death, his dad had given him and his sister the half-developed resort hotel. His sister, an ICU nurse, had come up with the idea of turning it into a clinic that served the local community and helped people like their mum, whose parents had both died of malaria—a disease that was easily curable with access to proper medical care. Care they'd been unable to afford. Noah had suggested it also treated tourists, so that there'd be a steady revenue stream. Then he'd left his sister to it.

'I just—' He stopped.

'What?'

Rebecca gave his hand a squeeze. Sympathy he didn't deserve.

'I did what I always do. Stuck my head in the sand and told myself that I was doing the right thing by staying in Sydney, working my ass off to buy fancy equipment so volunteer surgeons could come in and perform lifesaving surgeries for people who deserved them.'

'The clinic's got amazing resources because of all your hard work,' Rebecca insisted.

'I should have been here,' Noah said, in a voice he barely recognised.

He should have been here helping his sister. Being a good big brother. Helping her and her husband with the clinic, their children—all of it. And then, very possibly, they might not have been on that road, on that day, at the moment that idiot had raced down the switchbacks and driven their car off the road and into a ravine.

Rebecca took a deep breath. 'Want to know what I've been telling myself these past few weeks?'

He gave her a soft, teasing smile. 'That the universe will sort it all out for you?'

She gave him a *ha-ha-very-funny* look, then softened. 'A little bit that, but mostly I've been thinking how the only way I can change things in the past is by living proactively in the present.'

'That sounds very philosophical for a woman who comes prepared with three hairbands on her wrist at all times.'

They both looked at her wrist where, sure enough, there were spare hairbands. She took the light-hearted jibe and ran with it. 'Living in the present doesn't have to mean not being prepared for it. It's more…' She shifted her legs round so that she was facing him. 'The fact that you didn't shut this place down the day your sister died means something.'

Noah tipped his head in affirmation. 'Go on.'

'I think you believe that the work done here is important.'

'Of course.'

'And, if I'm right, you also believe it honours your mother's legacy. She sounds like she was a caring, loving woman, who put her family first.'

'That was her, all right. She was the essence of maternal love.'

Rebecca's smile softened. 'You're fortunate to have had that.'

He was. It was something Rebecca hadn't had, and he saw what she was trying to point out. He should be grateful for what he *had* had, not for what he hadn't. Which did mean maybe the clinic could be run in a different way. Right now it didn't need more fancy machines. It needed someone who cared at the helm.

Rebecca gave him another thoughtful look, then asked, 'If you decided to stay here, how much would you be leaving behind in Sydney?'

He could've laid out all the facts. Told her how he was regularly wooed by elite hospitals across Australia and beyond. How he was requested by name by the country's biggest sports stars and often invited to restaurant openings and other high society events. But there was a flipside to that lifestyle. The absence of any time for socialising. His lack of interest in anything beyond a casual relationship. The occasional dark nights of the soul when he'd wonder what the hell he was doing with his life and, worse, whether or not he would end up alone if he continued in this vein.

He looked Rebecca in the eye and, trusting in their friendship said, 'Beyond a couple of unopened bottles of beer in a fridge in a soulless bachelor pad, not much.'

It was a stark admission. He did love his job. But he could do it here just as easily. And without the pressure of television interviews with sports stars and tech gurus, and all the other high-profile patients the hospital regularly dangled in front of him more for their kudos than his professional satisfaction, he'd have that feeling he enjoyed with every patient he treated here in Bali, because he was giving precisely the type of care his mother would have loved to have given in her name.

'Are you sure you didn't also study psychology?' he asked.

Rebecca rolled her eyes. 'Let's just say I've been asking myself a lot of deep and meaningful questions lately. I've just turned that looking glass on to you to see if it helps.'

'It has.' He smiled and then, as if it was the most natural thing in the world, swept the backs of his fingers along her cheek, as if she were a girlfriend or a lover.

She flushed under his touch.

The energy between them surged and grew thick with promise. 'You've been a good friend to me,' he said.

She looked down, her dark lashes brushing against her cheeks. When she lifted her eyes up to meet his again, they were glistening.

Something that felt like hope gave a fist-pump in his chest. Was this what it was like to meet your kindred spirit? To meet The One?

Just as quickly the fist bashed into his conscience.

What could he offer her?

Friendship. He wanted something more, but the two little girls waiting for him a few hundred metres away were his reminder that he was not in a place to make promises. What if she wanted children of her own? He had no idea where he stood on that. Not with the plates he was spinning.

'Is that what we are?' she asked. 'Friends?'

The air between them hummed with anticipation. 'I'm not sure what we are,' he answered honestly.

His eyes stayed locked to hers for a moment and then, as if summoned, dropped to her lips.

He'd been wanting to pull her into his arms and make good on his instinct to kiss her ever since he'd met her. A primitive indicator that friendship wasn't all he was after.

'I'd like to be friends,' he said, tugging his eyes back up to meet hers. 'You say things I need to hear. And I would hate for that to stop for any reason.'

His eyes dropped to her lips again, practically spelling out what he wasn't saying. If they made this relationship physical he was giving no guarantees that he'd be able to see it through into a relationship.

Rebecca cleared her throat and, obviously feeling awkward, made a one-eighty change in conversation. 'I know I'm supposed to be flipping coins and leaving stuff up to the universe to make decisions for me, but if you're genuinely struggling with which way to go—Sydney or staying here—sometimes I find writing lists really helps clear things up for me. You know—putting stuff in black and white.'

He laughed and tipped an invisible cap. 'On your advice, I will sit down tonight to make one.'

He knew what the first item should be: *Don't fall in love.*

He rose and pointed to the phone by her side. 'I'm afraid my woes have steered us off track. Weren't we trying to figure out what's going on with your grandmother?'

Rebecca went ashen at the reminder. 'Nanny Bea! Sorry. I've got to ring her again.' She threw him a pleading look. 'Do you mind staying while I ring? Just in case—you know….'

Just in case something was wrong.

The vulnerability of her request wrapped round his heart. 'Not at all.'

She thumbed an app open. 'Oh! She's sent a text message.' She pressed a button, her brows arrowing together and then, just as quickly, flying up to her forehead. 'Oh, my goodness!' She turned the phone towards him, her face wreathed in smiles. 'Nanny Bea's been on a date!'

He pressed his hands to his chest, as if he'd been struck by an arrow, then dropped them when Rebecca began to frown at the message. 'What?'

'It's just a bit weird, that's all.' She tried to put on a smile but didn't entirely succeed. 'But I guess this is more evidence that the world works in mysterious ways.' She frowned again and added, almost to herself, 'I guess even if the universe gives us things it's still up to us to decide what to do about them.'

Yes, thought Noah, his fingers finding the coin he'd kept in his pocket ever since Rebecca had tossed it to him. *It certainly is.*

CHAPTER NINE

'BYE, NAN. HAVE fun and be safe. Love you.'

After a wave and an air-kiss, Rebecca ended the video call, slipped her phone into the pocket of her backpack and gave Noah at not entirely apologetic smile.

'Sorry about that. Just doing my daily check-in.' She rubbed her hands together in a show of excitement. 'Okay! Let's go and see this monkey temple.'

It was a Saturday afternoon. When the girls had joined Rebecca at the pool for a morning swim—something they'd taken to doing most mornings before school—they'd discovered that Rebecca hadn't yet been to the Sacred Monkey Sanctuary.

The girls had run back to the villa and dragged Noah out to the pool, along with a pile of notebooks so he could make a list of all of the places they thought Rebecca should see, and then they'd insisted he take them all out.

So here they were, backpacks filled with sun-block and water, all set to head off to the sanctuary. It was the closest to a family outing Rebecca had ever had as an adult, and it was impossible not to remember the moment when the girls had asked Noah if she was his girlfriend. And then, of course, the moment he'd made it very clear that she was in The Friend Zone.

'Everything all right at home?' Tiny lines of concern fanned out from Noah's eyes.

'I don't think I've ever heard Nan so happy,' Rebecca admitted, smiling her thanks to Noah who, gentleman that he was, had just opened the Jeep's passenger door for her. The girls were already in the back, ready for their outing. When Noah had climbed into the driver's seat she continued. 'She and Nathan are off to visit an art gallery.'

Nathan Parker was her Nan's new beau. A widower and retired civil engineer, Nathan had moved to the seaside to be near his daughter and grandchildren. The pair had met at the library, when they'd each reached for the same copy of *Jane Eyre* and it had been, according to her Nan, love at first sight.

'It's a bit further down the coast from her village and it's rumoured to have the best tearoom in Cornwall. Apparently, the carrot cake is to die for.'

'Are they going for the art or the cake?' Noah asked as he pulled his own door shut and clicked his safety belt into place, after triple-checking that the girls had done the same.

Her heart gave a little squeeze. He was obviously trying not to smother the girls with protective measures, but clearly had a safety-first checklist going on in his head. Bless him… She adored the girls, but she could also see insta-parenting from Noah's perspective. Panic-inducing. Proper 'in at the deep end' stuff.

It did make her wonder… Would he ever want children of his own or, now that he had the girls, was he drawing a line under that possibility? The fact he'd properly Friend Zoned her probably meant she should make her hormones do the same. She wanted children. At least the option to try. But if it didn't work she was open to other options.

Sensing Noah's gaze on her, Rebecca made herself laugh and continue in a light-hearted tone. 'My grandmother is a very competitive cake-maker. If she hears someone else is offering cakes to die for she'll drive from one end of Britain to the other to investigate.'

'What is carrot cake?' Isla asked. 'Does it taste like supper or dessert?'

Noah glanced into the rear-view mirror. 'Didn't your mum ever make it for you?'

Both girls shook their heads.

'What about Lamingtons?' he asked. 'Our mum used to make them for us all the time. Did she make those?'

Again, two dark haired heads shook back and forth.

'What *did* she make for you?'

'Mummy didn't cook,' Isla said matter-of-factly. 'She said she was like you, Uncle Noah.'

'Oh?' He shot Rebecca a mystified look. 'And what is that, exactly?'

Ruby piped up. 'Mummy said you could burn water.'

Rebecca stifled a laugh. Obviously his culinary skills were better than that. The barbecue had been delicious.

Noah pretended to look hurt. 'I'm sure I could manage something slightly better than burnt water. It's just—I've never really allowed time for cooking.' He tightened his hands round the steering wheel and pressed his arms out to their full length, as if creating space between himself and the memories.

Almost to himself, he explained, 'My mum—your grandmother—was an amazing cook. She despaired at the two of us, always trying and failing to get us to cook with her.'

When he fell silent Rebecca volunteered, 'I was pretty much tied to my nan's apron strings.'

Noah shot her a quick forlorn smile. 'Mum always conceded to whatever things my father wanted, and us learning how to cook wasn't one of them. We were always doing sport, or going to some sort of after-school club. She did try.'

He laughed quietly, but Rebecca could tell it wasn't because his memories were happy.

'There was one time she tried to get me in the kitchen with her when I was home from med school. She insisted learning to make her nasi goreng was the way I'd win a wife. Suffice it to say her cunning plan didn't work.' He held up his left hand and wiggled his empty ring finger at her.

Rebecca studied him as he fixed his gaze on the road. She was pretty sure Noah's lack of cooking skills was not the reason why he was single.

A cloud of sadness hung over him as he navigated the vehicle out of the village and drove deeper into the island, where the road was shrouded by thick jungle canopy.

Isla said, 'Mummy always took us to the bakery if we wanted anything. She said that was what bakeries were for.'

'Daddy made us Laklak cakes once,' Ruby reminded her.

'They were burnt,' Isla said sombrely, and

then, to Rebecca's astonishment, they both began to giggle at the memory.

Noah and Rebecca exchanged a look. It was the first time Rebecca had known the girls to openly talk about their parents and not get tearful. Noah looked panicked. Rebecca instantly understood. He wanted it to continue, but didn't know how.

She twisted in her seat as much as the seatbelt would allow and asked, 'What's a Laklak cake?'

The girls grinned and spoke over one another, explaining about cakes made of rice flour that they were small—like the size of their hands, not Noah's—and how, depending upon where you got them, they came with grated coconut or sweetened condensed milk. They were often bright green and, most of all, they were delicious even if they were burnt.

'They do sound delicious,' Rebecca said. 'Noah, what do you think? Could we hunt down some Laklak cakes on the way to the monkey temple?'

He threw her a grateful look. 'Sounds perfect. Let's do it.'

They proceeded to have one of the most perfect afternoons Rebecca had ever had.

Fuelled by the delicious coconutty cakes they'd found at a roadside bakery, they went to the Sacred Monkey Sanctuary. When they saw how huge it was Isla grabbed Noah by the hand and Ruby did the same to Rebecca. The girls insisted that Noah and Rebecca hold hands as well as they walked round the vast sanctuary.

'We don't want anyone to get lost,' Ruby said gravely.

So, Noah held out his hand to Rebecca and she took it.

'Is this all right?' he asked as he wove his fingers through hers.

'Fine,' she squeaked.

It wasn't just all right—it was perfection. She felt contented, in a way she'd never imagined possible. As if she'd come home. It made her wonder if home could actually be a person—not a place.

She'd been so intent on setting up the GP surgery in Cornwall she hadn't stopped to consider if it was a place that would make them both happy. With her hand in Noah's she felt safe in a way she hadn't in years. Not that being raised by her nan or that any of her other relationships had been frightening. Far from it. It was more that she'd always felt as if her young life had been a quest to create the one thing that was missing: a big, happy, family.

And here on this day, in this place—even though she knew it wasn't really true—she felt like she was part of one. They laughed at silly things. Noticed who'd left a pocket of their backpack unzipped. And Noah was the one who, as they were approaching a group of monkeys, suggested she twist her thick hair into a bun, so that the monkeys didn't make a grab for it.

'It's very beautiful,' he said, his eyes not quite meeting hers as he spoke. 'Monkeys are renowned for wanting beautiful things.'

A warm glow lit in her. A tiny flicker of hope that maybe one day this friendship could bloom into something else.

She unearthed a few hairpins from her bag, and the girls made a big show of tucking them all into place, then standing back and waiting for Noah's approval—which, to their combined satisfaction, he gave.

All tiny little building blocks that created the strong, safe, foundation of a family.

Though the girls had soon forgotten their insistence that they all hold hands, Noah reached out for hers and gave it a squeeze as the girls closed their eyes shut tight to make wishes and flip coins into the Holy Spring Temple Pool. 'You okay?'

She smiled at him. 'More than okay.'

The rest of the world blurred as they continued to look into one another's eyes. Someone jostled against Noah, pushing him closer to Rebecca. He wrapped a protective arm around her as he regained his balance.

'You okay?' he asked again as her hands landed on his chest.

She looked up at him, her heart-rate spiking as their gazes synced. She parted her lips to say something, but couldn't. How could she explain to him that from the moment she'd laid eyes on him she'd known he would always be more than a friend to her? That when he touched her she felt more alive than she had seconds earlier? That he could trust her to love the girls as much as he did even if trusting felt like stepping off a cliff into the great unknown?

She had no idea why, but the way he was looking at her made her feel as if he was thinking exactly same thing: *I want you...but I don't know how to begin.*

'Rebecca!' Isla grabbed her free hand and gave it a tug. 'Want to make a wish?'

'I do,' she whispered, her eyes still locked on Noah's.

Her wish ran through her head on a loop. *Fall in love with me. Fall in love with me. Fall in love with me.*

His hands shifted so that they rested loosely on her hips, as casually as if he'd done it a thousand times before and would a thousand times again. If he were to tip his head down to hers...

'What're you wishing for?' he asked.

This, she thought. *This and so much more.*

'Can't tell you,' she said, still close enough to kiss him. 'Otherwise it might not come true.'

'Well, then…' Noah locked her lips with a twist of his fingers. 'Better not say a word.'

Noah grimaced as he punched the 'accept' symbol on his phone. 'Hey, Dad. What's up?'

It was a curt greeting for a bereaved father. Not that his father had won any prizes for parenting over the years, or shown all that much heartache that his only daughter had had her life cut short—but still… Noah was the only blood relative he had left. He should do better.

'How's it going?' he asked, and then, after getting a neutral 'Fine…' that didn't really send the conversation anywhere, he asked about his father's wife.

'Ah, yes…about her…'

His father said something about his wife 'developing other interests'—which, Noah had learnt, was code for the marriage being over.

He felt the wind leave his chest. Wow. He really was all his father had left now.

Two bachelors and two little girls were all that remained of the Cameron clan.

He glanced over at the kitchen, where Rebecca was teaching the girls how to make a simple pasta dish. He felt himself soften as he took in the scene, barely hearing his father as he said something about being in the area—Singapore first, then somewhere else.

'So I thought I'd pop over to Bali after.'

'After what?'

'Jakarta, son. I just said.'

Skeins of guilt lanced through him. He'd just done to his father what his father had done to Noah as a boy. Pretended to listen while thinking of something else. With his father it had always been business, bank accounts, and whatever girlfriend he'd had on the go.

For Noah it was—

Hell. He let out a low whistle. He was being distracted by the simple but powerful joy of being part of something bigger than himself. A makeshift family. If that was what you could call it.

To be honest, it scared the hell out of him to put a label on it.

Ever since they'd started working their way through the girls' 'must-see' list for Rebecca, he'd felt more and more as if he, the girls and Rebecca were a unit. A foursome who worked better as a whole. No one tried to make anyone be anything they weren't. Noah wasn't their father. Rebecca wasn't their mother. And yet with the care they offered one another, and the compassion, it felt exactly like what he imagined being part of a 'real' family would.

But there was a part of him that worried he was leaning into Rebecca's ease with the children just to lighten his own load. Again, something his father had always done. Leaving 'women's work' to someone else. But this was different. Noah was the one who hated being left out. He loved being part of the foursome. The one they all picked on and teased. The one who brought a blush to Rebecca's cheeks with little more than a glance. The one who, despite it being a horrendous idea, was falling in love.

'Son?' His father's voice broke the silence.

'Yeah, sorry. You were saying?'

'I was saying I've booked a flight to Bali so I can have a talk with you.'

'Oh.' He couldn't think of anything he'd like less. His father's arrival would be like throwing a stone at the fragile new existence they'd formed. 'Right.'

'Don't worry, mate.' He could practically see his father rolling his eyes. 'I think you'll like what I'm going to propose. It should help you in your...you know...your circumstances.'

He was about to say, *No, Dad, what situation?* Just to get him to acknowledge that his granddaughters didn't have parents any more. But getting into a shouting match with his father had never solved anything.

'Fair enough. When will we see you?'

'We?' His father crowed. 'So you've found yourself a little lady to look after the girls, then? About time, son. A nanny with benefits. I'm impressed... I wondered how you were going to sort out that little situation.'

'Situation?' He barely kept the contempt out of his voice. 'I'd hardly call it that.'

'Call it what you like, son. It wasn't what you were born to.'

Noah's eyes flicked to Rebecca and the girls. They were stirring something on the stove, giggling away about who knew what. It looked fun. He wanted to be there. Be part of the fun. But his dad's words felt like a stark reminder that, of all the people his sister could have asked to be the girls' guardian, he was the least likely candidate. He wasn't a dad. A husband. He barely knew how to refer to the girls when they were out. They weren't his daughters. They were simply a legally binding unit. One Rebecca was not a part of.

'There's no one,' he said, wanting to dead-end his father's inaccurate and antiquated views on women. 'I meant me and the girls.'

But it hurt to omit Rebecca from the equation. He told himself the white lie was to protect her from his dad's presumptions. But the truth was he knew he was protecting his own heart. He couldn't just assume that Rebecca, who was nursing a broken heart of her own, would take him on, and the girls, not to mention a clinic that was a far cry from the children's hospital where she'd worked back in the UK. Maybe he'd move to Sydney. Maybe stay here. There were a million 'maybes' in his future, and that wasn't fair on her.

For all he knew, Rebecca was still planning on using that plane ticket of hers. He could ask her, of course. Ask her what she really wanted. But the truth was he didn't want to know. Not just yet. The part of him that was still reeling from his sister's death wanted this…whatever it was…to have a bit more time.

'Whatever you say, son. If you want to be PC about it, go for it,' his father continued. 'But you and I both know you will not be getting back on the work horse in Sydney without a woman by your side. Paid or otherwise. You're like me. Not built for it—the whole parenting lark. Heaven knows what your sister was thinking when she picked *you* as the girls' guardian.'

Bloody hell! He turned his back on the cosy scene in the kitchen and strode out deeper into the gardens.

'I don't really think you're in the best place to judge what I'm capable of, Dad.'

His father whistled. 'Ooh! So he *can* fight back.'

'Seriously? You want me to fight with you about whether or not I can look after the girls?'

'You've been faffing about there for three months, son. Reputations have been gained and lost in less time. You've got to get yourself back to Sydney. Remind people who you are. What would your mother think if you let yourself down like this? Let the Cameron name disappear without so much as a whimper?'

Noah grunted as if he'd been physically punched. His father really knew how to swing hard with the low blows.

At least Noah was here. *Trying.* Yanking the girls out of their comfort zone would be a last resort option for him. The girls were in their school, their home, in the only country they'd ever really known.

And it wasn't exactly as if his father was in any place to cast aspersions. He'd flown in to Bali, holding his Panama hat to his chest as his daughter's ashes were absorbed into the sea, then jumped on the earliest plane out, leaving Noah to deal with the aftermath of a horrific situation. One that should've cut any normal father to the bone.

'What does your boss make of this, son? This leave of absence you've taken?'

'She's not got a problem with it.'

'*She?*' His father hooted. 'What? Does she have you on one of those "compassionate leave" stints? Let me tell you, son…that'll come back to bite you in the ass.'

Noah tuned his father out. He'd had this lecture enough times during his childhood to be able to recite it by rote. *Win at sport. Excel at school. Never rely on anyone. Be king of whatever mountain you climb.*

It was the Aussie male form of encouragement.

Or was it time he called a spade a spade?

It was bullying disguised as parenting.

Even *thinking* it felt too close to the bone.

He took a mental swing at the thought and bashed it out of his mind.

'Right, Dad. Gotta go. Text me your flight details and I'll send a car.'

'There's a good lad.'

Noah hung up the call.

He walked back into the kitchen once he'd shaken off his rage.

Rebecca looked over. 'Everything all right?'

'Yup. My father's coming for a visit in a couple of weeks.'

'Oh!' Rebecca's face lit up. 'That's great news.'

He tried to get his expression to match hers, but knew he was failing. She was clearly waiting for an invitation to meet him, but there was no chance he was going to subject her to that man.

She gave the girls some quiet instructions and then, clearly sensing he wasn't over the moon, crossed to him, her smile tipping at the edges. 'It *is* good news, right?'

He caught the stream of insults he could have unleashed and said, 'Yeah. It'll be good for him to see the girls.'

Rebecca's smile faltered. She understood what he was saying. She wasn't invited.

He was about to explain about his dad, and how he wanted to set him straight on a few things before he met her, but Rebecca beat him to it.

'Right, then. Well… How about you come and look at what the girls have magicked up? You just need to sprinkle some of these herbs on top and you can sit down and enjoy.'

'You're not staying?'

She gave him a wide-eyed look. 'I don't think that's a good idea. Do you?'

Noah knew what she was really asking. What was he playing at? Letting her into their day-to-day lives, but not inviting her to meet his father? From her point of view it was a big slight. Family meant everything to her.

He reached out and took her hand in his. 'Please. Stay for dinner. We'd like it.'

'We?' she asked, eyebrows raised.

'Me,' he answered honestly. 'I'd like it. You already know the girls would have moved you in weeks ago if they could.'

He hoped she knew what he was really saying. That he cared for her, but he needed time.

She looked down, then up. 'I don't know, Noah. It's—'

'It's *dinner*,' he finished for her. 'Please stay. And tomorrow we'll talk. I'll explain about my dad.'

She let the comment simmer between them for a moment and then, when the girls called her to check on the dish, she gave him a conditional smile. 'I'll stay for the girls. For dinner.'

The decision was a premium display of her strength of character. He could tell he'd hurt her, and yet she'd put those feelings to the side for the girls. And, with any luck, for him. She deserved more from him. He owed her a decision, one way or another.

He gave her hand a light caress, then lifted it to his lips, giving the back of it a soft kiss. 'Thank you.'

She stiffened, and then, to his surprise, relaxed and laughed. 'You make disliking you very difficult.'

'You want to *dislike* me?'

To be fair, he didn't blame her. Flirty one minute. Distant the next. Welcoming her into the family home and then shutting the door in her face. He wouldn't like himself very much if he were in her shoes.

'I don't want to get hurt again,' she said honestly. 'But maybe that's not how life works. Maybe it's pain that makes us stronger. Come on.' She hooked her arm and gestured for him to follow her. 'It's best when it's hot.'

After she'd turned to the girls he put his hand in his pocket, his fingers catching on the British coin that had already decided so much. In his heart he knew he was well past the point of leaving his fate up to a flip of a coin. It was time to make a decision.

CHAPTER TEN

REBECCA SHOOK HER finger at her telephone screen. 'You make sure he gets you home at a respectable hour, young lady.'

Her nan, whom she'd video called a few minutes earlier, giggled as if Rebecca had just told her not to ride home on a unicorn. 'Don't you worry about that, love. We're in our seventies—not seventeen!'

'So long as you're sensible,' Rebecca continued with mock authority. 'Otherwise I'll have to fly home and chaperone.'

'Rebecca Stone! Have I taught you nothing? I don't want you even *thinking* about leaving that lovely tropical island of yours,' her nan chided, with her own well-practised finger-wag. 'I've not seen you look this happy in actual years.'

Rebecca was about to protest, but as she caught a glimpse of Noah, moving from one patient's cubicle to another, and felt the increasingly familiar rush of tingles course through her, she knew deep down that her nan was right. She was happy.

Sure, things were weird with Noah. She didn't just fancy him. She cared for him. She was pretty sure he felt the same way, too. But if this was the universe gifting them to one another the universe's timing was awful.

She'd only come out of a wretched long-term relationship a few months ago. How on earth was she ready to fall in love again?

And as for Noah...

Falling in love whilst grieving for his sister and trying to be a parent... How would that work?

She nipped the thought in the bud. Shifting from friends to lovers was her fantasy and hers alone.

At best, this was an intense holiday friendship that she was endowing with way too much meaning. As for expecting an invitation to meet his dad...? What had she been thinking?

Hormones.

For sure.

Her tummy felt like a butterfly sanctuary whenever she was near Noah.

Nothing, however, compared to what her nan was experiencing. At long last her grandmother had met her perfect match. Nathan. Her septuagenarian stallion, she called him. And after thirty-three years of widowhood, heaven knew she deserved to meet someone.

It had been just two weeks since Nan had met Nathan. And in that short period of time, they'd gone from being 'two old codgers' who enjoyed one another's company to 'a silver fox and a vixen' who were, by their own admission, madly in love.

If she weren't so charmed by it, Rebecca thought, she might be a tiny bit envious. Things with Noah weren't nearly as straightforward.

Yes, he'd said they would talk, but that had been days ago, and each time they'd sat down something or someone had aborted it. Although their friendship had definitely built in strength, and that meant the world to her. If she really wanted to do right by him she should draw a line in the sand for him. Tell him it was friends or nothing.

If only her body wasn't head over heels in lust with him.

'Dr Stone?' The charge nurse handed Rebecca a tablet with her next patient's information up on the screen, then pointed to a cubicle.

'Oh, love!' Nanny Bea chided. 'Are you keeping patients waiting just to gossip with your lovestruck nan?'

'Not at all,' Rebecca protested. 'It's important to make sure my lovestruck nan is behaving sensibly.'

Her grandmother tsked away the notion. 'I'm perfectly fine, and if there's any time to lose my marbles for a handsome man who treats me like a queen, it's now.' She grinned mischievously. 'Take it from me, love. Losing your marbles over someone who treats you like a queen is worth it at any time in life.' She made a shooing gesture. 'Go on. Don't keep your patients waiting on my account.'

Rebecca blew her nan a kiss then ended the call, still smiling as she pulled back the curtain to see her next patient.

The second she laid eyes on the little boy in the cubicle, she knew what the problem was.

Gastroenteritis.

His lips were dry. His eyes had a sunken look. And one glance at his body language showed he was both irritable and lethargic.

'Finally!' his mother cried over Rebecca's introduction. 'We've been waiting for twenty minutes.'

Rebecca smiled apologetically, then stepped into the cubicle, pulling the curtain behind her. The clinic was obviously busy, but parents were always stressed in situations like this. Even at the best of times—at home with a familiar doctor. On holiday, she was quickly learning, that tension was doubled. They were frightened about language barriers, different treatment methods, substandard care practices—none of which they'd have to worry about here in this clinic. Or anywhere on Bali for that matter.

She and Noah had taken a child down to the main hospital the other day, for some special-ised scans, and the facilities there were marvel-lous. What had surprised her, when he'd circled around the back of the hospital, had been the *very* fancy private wing he'd pointed out. The one where foreigners discreetly dipped in for a bit of a holiday nip and tuck holiday.

She'd heard about places like it, of course, but had never come face to face with one. From what she'd seen there were a fair few people who'd be returning home extolling the 'rejuvenating effects' of their holiday.

She sat down on her wheeled stool, and after a quick round of questions with the mum, to as-certain where they were from—Holland—where they were staying in Bali—a resort down the road—what they'd been eating and any activi-ties they'd been up to, she turned her attention to the boy, gave him a soft smile and introduced herself.

Before he could say his name, she felt her stool

begin to move across the floor. The low murmur of voices around the clinic rose in volume.

Aftershock. Must be. There had been an earthquake earlier that morning which, mercifully, hadn't taken any lives. It had left their part of the island unscathed, but she knew the main hospital an hour or so south of them couldn't take any extra patients as they were dealing with a bit of structural damage to their casualty unit.

She held out her hand to shake the little boy's. 'That was interesting, wasn't it?' She smiled.

Hmm... Her comment hadn't really registered. She held his hand in hers. It was cool, but not cold, which was good. His skin was pale, but not mottled. Also good. She'd run a few more tests before deciding whether or not to put him on an IV drip. Sometimes a steady intake of rehydration solution did the trick.

She kept hold of his hand, wanting to check for capillary refill. 'I'm just going to give your finger a bit of a squeeze to see how fast your body responds, all right?'

He nodded, a vacant look in his eyes. Poor little chap was exhausted. She pressed until the blood left the tip of his fingers then released. A normal finger would've bounced back straight away. Johann's didn't.

Unfortunately, gastroenteritis—or, as tourists often referred to it, Bali Belly—wasn't uncommon in foreign visitors, and it looked as if this poor lad was no exception.

'Johann's been sick for four days now,' the mother said with a crisp note of displeasure. 'All those surf lessons we pre-booked—wasted.' She fixed her gaze on Rebecca. 'I tell him to wash his hands a thousand times a day, and to stay away from food he can't identify. But does he listen? No.'

Rebecca bit her tongue. This sort of comment arose with surprising frequency amongst parents who were frustrated that their children's illness had somehow ruined their holiday. Rebecca had always thought the whole point of coming to a place like this was to experience new things. Try new things.

Like falling in love with an emotionally unavailable ninja surgeon and his two little girls?

Unbidden, an image of Noah piggybacking both girls round the garden yesterday as they all played tag sprang to mind. They always had such fun together. They'd always organically find themselves gathering at the end of the day for a bit of a giggle…and then something else would always happen. A spark of connection. A moment of physical contact. Something that tugged her and Noah together then pushed them apart—as if they both knew that whatever it was they shared was short term.

She cornered the thought and stuffed it behind a mental door, then took a slow breath and made a few notes on the tablet she'd been given for the patient's records.

The mother tapped at the screen to get Rebecca's attention. 'I gave him vodka yesterday and this morning, on the recommendation of one of the other guests.'

'Sorry?' She had Rebecca's attention now. Not only was Johann seven years old—vodka was *not* a cure for gastroenteritis.

The woman explained, as if to a child, that she'd had it on *excellent* authority from another guest at their hotel that a shot of vodka every morning was the answer, and if that didn't work a beer. She was a nurse, the woman told her. Swore by it.

Rebecca tipped her head to one side and as neutrally as she could said, 'Rehydrating is very important, and whilst many adults like to think alcohol will kill any bacterial bugs they may have picked up the infection could be viral, so not "killable" as such. Also, alcohol dehydrates.' She managed to dial back a very sharp reprimand about the dangers of giving a child alcohol and closed with a simple sentence. 'As a paediatric doctor, I wouldn't recommend it—ever.'

'This vodka had electrolytes,' the woman countered vehemently, stepping towards Rebecca. She glanced at Rebecca's left hand which, of course, was ring-free. 'I know my child. Someone who doesn't have children wouldn't ever understand the risks you're prepared to take to look after them.'

Ouch. Well, that certainly stung. Less so, seeing as she'd spent over a decade of her life training to be a paediatric surgeon, but…the woman had chosen a target and hit it.

Rebecca said nothing, which only seemed to enrage the woman more. Rebecca put her hands up between them and took a step back, just dodging the finger now poking in her face.

'I'm not a bad mother.'

This was another pronouncement Rebecca encountered a lot. Along with defensiveness. Bullying. Insistence that they were good parents. It was stress, she reminded herself.

She's belittling you to make herself feel big because she's frightened.

'The vodka I gave him,' the mother continued, 'was *electrolyte* enhanced. Same stuff as all those fancy drinks down at the pharmacy, and we didn't even need to leave the hotel.'

Rebecca looked the woman straight in the eye. 'Two million children a year die from gastroenteritis. It was a wise decision to bring your son here.'

The mum all but choked on her rage. She knew Rebecca wasn't giving her a compliment.

Rebecca regretted having spoken so sharply, but seriously… Vodka? Here in Bali, an island geared towards tourism, it was simple to get a doctor to come to a hotel. It was a service they offered themselves at the clinic. Not to mention the fact that any member of hotel staff would happily go to the pharmacy for you. Why choose electrolyte-enhanced vodka designed for party hounds to 'cure' your seven-year-old child?

She returned to her examination of the boy, reminding herself that she didn't know the whole picture. Perhaps this lady was a single mum, on holiday for the first time and feeling out of her element. Perhaps she'd saved for years for this break and now that she was here, all her efforts felt ruined. At least she'd come to the clinic…

As she took Johann's temperature and pulse, a commotion sounded down at the intake area. Noah was paged on the Tannoy. She heard footsteps running past.

His?

Focus!

'Have you been able to keep anything down, Johann? Any fluids?'

'It all comes right back up,' the mother answered for him. 'Or out, if you know what I mean.'

Rebecca gave her a polite nod. 'Any blood in the stools?'

The mother recoiled. 'I didn't look at it!'

Rebecca pulled her stethoscope from around her neck and gave Johann a smile. 'I'm going to have a listen to your tummy, all right?'

The boy let out a sigh and flopped back onto the immaculate white pillow. He was knackered, poor thing.

Just as she popped the earpieces in, Noah stuck his head into the curtained area.

Her heart-rate quickened. No matter how frequently she saw him, each appearance elicited a new, fresh burst of attraction. As if someone had opened a cold bottle of fizzy drink inside her chest.

'Sorry to interrupt,' Noah said. 'But I'm going to need an extra pair of hands in the OR as soon as you're able. Up for it?'

Her pulse leapt, then hit that old familiar rhythm it used to have when she'd worked as a surgeon. A rhythm that slowed down time so that she could see, frame by frame, every move she had to make before she did it, ensuring the child brought into her care survived.

'Absolutely.'

She was about to ask what had happened when the irritable mother cut in, 'What about Johann?'

Despite a niggle that something seriously wrong must have happened—a worse after-shock somewhere else on the island, an incoming tsunami—she kept her voice calm.

'We're going to set Johann up on an IV drip. Get him rehydrated.' Rebecca informed her in her 'non-negotiable' voice. 'We'll also take stool and urine samples and give him an anti-emetic. It'll help settle his stomach enough to curb the vomiting.' Before the mum could interject again, Rebecca waved a colleague over. 'One of our nurses will sit here with you—this is Nurse Kartika.' To Johann she added, 'Her name means shining star and she has the personality to match.'

She quickly explained the situation to Kartika, then shared a complicit look with the nurse. International medical personnel silent speak for *Tread carefully. This one's a live wire.*

'She'll make sure a doctor checks over the results before he is released.'

There was shouting, and then the sound of a woman keening from towards the entrance to the clinic.

'And how long will all that take?' Johann's mother cried.

'An hour. Maybe two. It depends upon how your son's health is after treatment.' She fixed the mum with her steeliest gaze. 'That *is* why you brought him here? To make sure your son's condition doesn't worsen?'

The woman stared at her for a moment and then, completely unexpectedly, burst into tears. 'I'm sorry. I know I'm being horrid. It's just—' She lowered her voice and nodded at Johann. 'His new stepfather… This is supposed to be our honeymoon.' She flashed a very shiny diamond ring, then covered it as if she was ashamed to be wearing it. 'His new dad isn't the hugest fan of children, but he made an exception for Johann because he's usually such a good boy. Doesn't need to be shouted at. Do you Jo-Jo?'

She walked over to her son and gently stroked his blond fringe away from his forehead before planting a soft kiss on his cheek. She looked back up at Rebecca.

'I just— I'd made plans, you know? Jo-Jo was supposed to be being looked after by his father while we were on this trip, but of course he flaked. I'd made sure every single detail of this trip was going to be perfect, so Karl—that's my new husband—wouldn't have any reason to think he'd made a mistake in marrying me, and—'

'Am I the reason he made the mistake, Mummy?' Johann asked.

'No, darling. No, no, no.' The tears flowed

even more freely now as she pulled her son into her arms and held him close.

Rebecca's heart squeezed tight. The poor woman. And poor Johann. It didn't sound like a dream arrangement for any of them.

It wasn't as if Rebecca was in a place to give marital advice, but something told her she should take this as a sign that the collapse of her own relationship had actually been a blessing.

Something deep inside her shifted.

It was time to step away from the self-pity she'd been feeling about her broken engagement and start proactively walking towards her future.

One that involved Noah?

Another round of shouting and crying erupted at the far end of the clinic.

'I'm really sorry. I'm going to have to dash. But you're in good hands with Nurse Kartika.'

She took off at a jog towards the operating theatres.

Noah intercepted her just as she was about to enter the scrub room. 'Family of six riding a scooter involved in a car crash.'

She winced. She'd seen drivers precariously balance entire extended families on small motorcycles meant for one, maybe two people max. This wasn't going to be pretty. 'Was it the aftershock?'

He shook his head, confused. 'What after-shock?'

She was about to explain, then realised what-ever had been going on for him had trumped her feeling a bit of a wobble. 'I presume you need me to scrub in?'

'Yes. A four-by-four didn't stop at a junc-tion—smashed right into them.' He pushed the door to the scrub room open, and she saw a specialist nurse already preparing two sets of surgical gowns. 'They're doing CT scans now. Murray and Irawan are in the trauma units with two of them.'

She nodded. It was a fortunate time to have the extra volunteer surgeons on staff.

'Grandmother, dad, mother and three chil-dren aged four, two and an infant—all piled on, along with the family's shopping. No helmets.'

She sucked in a sharp breath as she ran a line of surgical solution along her nails. Noah's eyes snapped to hers. He would know she wasn't feel-ing the sting of the medicated soap. It was the knowledge of what was to come. Children rarely wore bike helmets here. Adults did—but not al-ways. Her heart was crumpling in on itself over that family, but she couldn't afford to let herself become emotional. Not with lives at stake.

'Grandmother is getting CPR. Dad has at least two compound fractures in his leg—took the brunt of the collision. Mum has a broken arm and suspected internal bleeding. I'll be seeing the two of them. The baby and the four and two-year-olds are getting scans, but you'll need to—'

'Wait. They're *all* here?' She knew they didn't have the resources to operate on everyone.

Noah's expression was grim. 'Also the driver of the car. After the earthquake the trauma centre at the main hospital has had to send everyone to other clinics and smaller hospitals. We're all that's left. And we were the closest. For whatever reason, today seems to be accident day. Lots of idiot drivers out on the road.'

His eyes darkened to a fathomless black. It was impossible to read if he was feeling rage or grief.

She wouldn't blame him for either, but knew there was no way he should go into surgery with either mindset. Sure, he'd lost his family to an idiot driver—but, as she'd just been reminded, it was best not to judge before you knew the whole story. Heck. If Noah had met her three months ago he would've thought she was a pathetic sloth who never left her bed.

'You can't enjoy the ups if you don't have the downs!'

Her grandmother's voice sing-songed through her head.

Nanny Bea's wisdom was usually pretty spot-on and today was no different.

'The driver?' she asked, wincing in advance of the answer.

'He had a stroke. Lost control. I've got Rahman and Nikolaides working on him.'

Ah. There you go. Not all drivers were idiots.

And if there was ever a good time for someone to have a stroke, now was it. Those two specialists had volunteered a few months back. Rahman was a vascular specialist and Nikolaides a neurosurgeon. They'd met at Cambridge years ago, and always promised each other they'd learn how to surf by the time they turned fifty. Last year they'd each celebrated their forty-ninth birthdays.

'Okay. Got it.' She turned off the tap with her elbow, hands raised as she prepared to glove up. 'I presume you have a masterplan?'

'All hands on deck. I'll see Dad and Mum in the next room. You'll see to the children in here.'

'All three?' Her eyes went wide.

'Unless you can magic some other surgeons out of the ether. We'll all pop in as and when we can.'

His tone was brusque, but the look in his eyes said something else altogether. It said he trusted her. He believed in her.

He stepped in close and leant in, his cheek

brushing against hers as he whispered in her ear. 'I'll be right next door.'

It was all the pep talk she needed.

Rebecca had survived busy days at work before. Eighteen-hour shifts at the hospital with only a few hours of snatched sleep. Twenty-four-hour days. Even less sleep. Junk food to fuel it all. A thousand broken dates with friends and would-be suitors. Little wonder she'd ended up with a doctor whose own schedule was just as busy.

The all-consuming demands of the job was one of the reasons she'd decided to step away from surgical work and into family practice, but from the moment she stepped into the clinic's operating theatre she felt a life-force surge through her that she hadn't experienced in years.

All three children had sustained severe road rash and other traumatic injuries.

The infant was the least harmed, though still badly hurt, despite having been cushioned in her mother's arms as the car crashed into them. Fractures to her tiny left arm. Possible whiplash. Cerebral bruising, but nothing to indicate an internal bleed. *Yet.* She'd need more scans, and an urgent consult from Nikolaides. Most pressingly, the tiny little girl had broken three ribs, one of which had caused a lung puncture.

As she called out preparatory instructions for

the other two children, Rebecca swiftly inserted a needle into the infant's pleural space to release the trapped air, then instructed a junior doctor visiting from Singapore to stay with her until the lung had been reinflated. When it was safe, she'd repair the injury to the lung tissue via the bronchial airways.

Much more seriously, the two-year-old and four-year-old boys had both sustained traumatic brain injuries. The eldest had a frightening skull fracture and the two-year-old had a depressed skull bone fracture. He'd also sustained a potentially lethal puncture wound. In his heart.

As she stepped towards the two-year-old's table an alarm sounded at the baby's table. Alarms had been sounding from the four-year-old's table from the moment he'd arrived.

She couldn't be in three places at once—but nor could she give up on any of these tiny lives. Panic began to rise from her gut to her chest. These children would need surgeries she hadn't performed in years. Could she remember the detailed procedures? Noah obviously believed in her, trusted her. And from a man like him, she had to believe it was trust well-placed.

She closed her eyes and allowed herself to count to one. These children didn't have time for her to make it all the way to ten. And then she got to work.

An hour later Noah pushed through the operating theatre door, holding a mask over his face.

Instead of saying what her heart was screaming—*It's so good to see you*—she said 'Aren't you meant to be operating?'

'Done the initial exams. They're both with the anaesthetist now. I'm just checking in.'

He might as well have told her he loved her for the comfort it gave her.

Was that what she wanted? For Noah to fall in love with her?

'Dr Stone?' her nurse prompted, handing her the scalpel.

'Yes. Sorry.' She began opening up the abdominal wall of the two-year-old, whose swollen tummy indicated...yup...massive internal bleeding.

'You okay?' Noah asked as multiple alarms began to sound.

'I will be when I can stem the flow...' She grabbed a few pads to soak up the excess blood, then snapped a small clamp into place. 'There!' She waited a moment, to ensure the clamp wouldn't put too much pressure on the other blood vessels around it. It stayed fixed. The big problem was going to be the piece of bamboo still in the little boy's heart. Ironically, or perhaps cruelly, it was probably the one thing keeping him alive.

She raised her eyebrows to him. 'I'm going to need Nikolaides in here. Is that possible?'

He nodded. 'Absolutely. Stroke victim wasn't as bad as he could've been. I'll send him in now. Will you need me?'

Alarms sounded at one of her other tables.

'We're losing him!'

She whipped around and saw the four-year-old's tiny body was seizing.

'Yes,' she said, almost to herself.

She'd need him. But not now. After.

This was one of those moments where her skill as a surgeon was all that stood between life and death for a child. And no matter how confident she was in her skills she already knew in her bones that not all of these children were going to make it out of here alive.

CHAPTER ELEVEN

'CLAMP.'

Noah's eyes were glued to the screen that was showing each of Rebecca's precise movements. She was clearly a surgeon at the top of her game, and he was impressed. His operations were finished, and he'd come in to assist her, but she didn't need his help. It was almost impossible to believe she hadn't done this type of surgery in over five years.

'You sure you haven't done this recently?' he asked.

'Like riding a bicycle,' she said grimly.

He didn't begrudge her the tone. She'd just called time of death on the four-year-old, whose internal injuries had proved too devastating to fix. Without being able to obtain the permission of his parents—both barely out of surgery themselves and still under anaesthetic—she had made the executive decision to use the boy's heart to replace the devastated remains of his little brother's.

It was the kind of decision he'd heard a handful of his army buddies talking about. Operating on one fallen comrade only to use their organs for someone else as a matter of urgency. War, natural disasters, car accidents—nothing about them was fair. And today was no different. But it felt different. And the reason was standing in front of him, lifting a small, perfect heart out of a chest that would never take a breath of life again.

'Scalpel.'

Rebecca had command of the operating theatre in a way he'd never borne witness to before. And he was pretty used to giving command performances himself. Not that that was the aim.

He could tell she wasn't doing this for the glory. And definitely not the pay cheque. There wasn't one.

No. Her entire aura was infused with respect for the life she'd just lost and the one she was hoping to save.

Her movements were gentle, deliberate. As if the boy was aware of them—which, of course, he couldn't possibly be. But Noah got it. She was honouring the four-year-old boy who would never laugh again, never cry, never be cuddled in his parents' arms again. She was honouring the reality that his loss of life meant he would be able to give the gift of it to his brother.

As he watched Rebecca he imagined his nieces reaching up to him, their small hands seeking comfort in his larger ones. His fingers balled into protective fists and then opened, feeling the gaping emptiness left behind.

The sensation all but cracked him in half. Enough to open up his brain and, more importantly, his heart to the message he clearly needed to receive: Life was too damn short to put living on hold. If he felt something for someone he was going to show it from now on. And by 'someone' he meant Rebecca.

After she'd placed the heart in a surgical bowl filled with ice, their eyes met. That increasingly familiar flare of heat he felt whenever they looked at one another all but scorched his own living, beating heart.

He kept his stance solid. His gaze unblinking. He wasn't going to shy away from the attraction they shared any more. Life was too precious. Too large a gift to fritter away on anything that didn't make him a better man.

'Right.' Rebecca was standing across from Noah at the two-year-old's table now. 'Let's give this heart a new home.'

Her eyes met his, and after a short nod of confirmation that they were both ready they began to prepare the area around the two-year-old's perforated heart, so that cardio-pulmonary by-pass could be initiated.

Once the cannulas and clamps were in place they removed the old heart, devastated by the clump of bamboo skewers he'd landed on when he'd been thrown from the Moto. The skewers had effectively become miniature spears, shredding the tiny heart beyond repair.

His brother's healthy heart was brought into place. The atmosphere in the room grew taut. If this failed, that would be two lives lost today.

Sensing the shift in mood, Rebecca brightened her voice and said, 'Let's see if my grandmother's attempts to teach me how to sew are up to the task.'

There was a murmur of laughter—the best sign of support from her team. They'd been watching her these last few hours and knew for a fact that her suturing was up to it.

Noah knew it was ridiculous, but he felt proud by proxy. The way a boyfriend might of his girlfriend. A husband of his wife.

He instantly took the thought and tried file it where he usually did—in the Do Not Revisit cupboard. But watching her replace a savaged heart with the new one made it impossible.

'I'll start with the left atrium...' She deftly stitched the four heart chambers into place, following suit with the ascending aorta. She removed the aortic cross clamp, and they all held their breath until…

Beep. Beep. Beep.

The soft crinkles around her eyes indicated that she was smiling. A chorus of cheers and sighs of relief filled the air. Losing one life had been devastating. Losing both would have been an unimaginable blow.

'Bravo, Dr Stone,' he said.

She blinked and drew in a sharp breath, as if she was about to admit something—something from the heart—but then said, 'Thank you for your help.'

Together they sutured the pulmonary artery, and the inferior and superior vena cavas to their corresponding valves. The heart was weaned from cardio pulmonary bypass. Using the echocardiogram, they ensured all the valves were functioning well, and that both of the ventricles were performing.

When she stepped back from the table after putting the final stitch in the boy's chest she said, 'Now comes the hard part.'

Freshly showered, Noah couldn't say he felt like a new man, but he knew they'd met the challenges of the day head-on and had done the best they could with a fraction of the staff a hospital would have had. And the worst part was over: telling the boys' parents.

He'd stood alongside Rebecca as she, at her own insistence, had informed the children's parents that two of their three children were in the ICU but that they'd been unable to save their eldest son. When they'd left the room she'd disappeared into the women's changing room before he could offer her a hug or a word of condolence.

He got it. Sometimes you needed to process things alone. But there were other times, like now, when you needed to know there was someone in your life who understood what you were going through.

Which was why he was waiting out here in the corridor.

When Rebecca eventually came out of the women's changing room her eyes snapped to his. She was clearly surprised to see him. She scanned him as if checking for damage, her eyes doing a double-take as they reached his shoulders.

'Your hair—' she said.

He gave his scalp a rough rub, and then, preprogrammed by his father's disapproving glares, made light of it. 'I know. Needs a cut.'

Rebecca frowned at him, confused by the comment. 'Why?'

'Not exactly surgery-friendly.'

'Plenty of surgeons have long hair.' She pointed at her own.

He shrugged, then pulled a swathe of it into his fist and feigned hacking it off with two of his fingers, more angry with himself for succumbing to his father's archaic stance than anything.

'Don't cut it,' she said. Her voice was lower than normal. As if the words had rasped up her throat against her will.

And just like that an image of a towel-clad Rebecca crashed into his head. She was playing with his hair. Combing her fingers through it, her face close to his as he gently tipped her chin up to see if a kiss would taste as good as he imagined it.

He shifted from one hip to the other. 'It's just about the same length as yours, I think.'

Seriously? That was all he had?

This new life plan of his to seize the day wasn't exactly turning him into a sparkling conversationalist.

She stared at him, then tugged her damp ponytail over her shoulder, studying it as if she'd never seen it before. 'I grew mine when I stopped doing surgery.'

Her voice carried a note of something he couldn't put his finger on. It wasn't regret, exactly…

Her eyes flicked back to his. 'I always wish I'd been braver.'

'Yeah. Me, too.'

He was pretty sure neither of them were talking about hair any more.

The air crackled between them—invisible bursts of electricity sweeping through parts of his body that would make wearing scrubs very awkward in about thirty seconds.

He wanted her. Now. And if he was reading the energy right she wanted him, too.

Making love to Rebecca Stone wasn't the sensible thing to do. But he'd done enough pragmatic thinking to last him a lifetime.

His toes practically curled with horror at his own ineptness as he heard himself say, 'The girls are asleep now. Would you like to come to mine for a cup of tea?'

What the hell? Since when had he turned into an idiot nineteen-year-old?

Rebecca looked at him askance, as if weighing up her options. 'Do you want tea?' she asked simply. 'Or me?'

And just like that all the blood in his brain crashed below his waistline.

The space between them evaporated, and before one more rational thought could enter his head they were kissing as if their lives depended upon it. Hungry, intense, exploratory kisses that doubled the shared energy surging between them.

Holding Rebecca in his arms felt like coming home. A feeling he'd never had with another woman. How could they know so little about one another's history and yet know in their guts that what they were doing was right? That moving their relationship to a physical level was a risk worth taking?

They knew enough, he told himself. *They knew what was important.*

He grabbed her hand and pulled her into a nearby examination room. 'Okay if I lock the door?'

She gave him a look that said, *It'd be foolish not to*, then reached across him to lock it herself. As she drew back her sweet scent filled his senses with burnt sugar and frangipani.

'Now, then…' She smiled. 'Where were we?'

He completely lost himself in her touch. Her caresses. The way she kissed. Soft and then urgent. Insatiable then teasing. It was like playing Russian roulette with his sanity. He'd never lost control with or for a woman before, but something about Rebecca made him believe he could trust her with everything. His body. His intellect. His heart.

But was the trust strong enough to risk his fragile new beginning with the girls?

As if she'd heard his thoughts she pulled away and pressed one of her hands against his chest, her fingers shifting softly against the fabric of his clean scrubs until she'd found what she'd been seeking. The racing beat of his heart.

'Do you want to go to them?' she asked, tipping her head in the direction of his villa.

He shook his head, then stopped to explain. 'I asked the sitter to stay with them overnight when I didn't know how long we'd be in the OR.'

She nodded, absorbing what the subtext of that was. *I'm free to be with you if that's what you want.*

They looked into one another's eyes, seeking answers, until he couldn't stand the distance between them any more. He dipped his head down and kissed her again.

'You taste as good as I imagined,' he whispered against her lips.

'You've imagined kissing me?' She nipped at his lower lip with her teeth, clearly emboldened by the admission.

'Don't sound so surprised.' He returned the gesture, pleased when it drew a mew of pleasure from her. He pulled back and gently shifted a few stray strands of hair off her cheek. 'Look at you… You've got to know you're sexy.'

Her bottom lip grated against her top teeth as her gaze dropped away from his.

Hell. Maybe she didn't. Well, that wouldn't do, would it? He tasked himself with showing her precisely how sexy she was.

He cupped her shoulders in his hands and waited until she met his eyes. 'I've wanted you from the moment I laid eyes on you, Dr Rebecca Stone.'

Her cheeks pinkened. 'I thought I was the only one carrying a flame.'

'No, you didn't,' Noah gently chastised.

She hadn't been the only one sending heated looks and she knew it. He'd also blatantly lied about that last coin toss. The one that had convinced her to stay. And he was pretty sure she knew it.

'There's been a fair amount of flirtation between the two of us over the past couple of weeks. And, though I know I've been wrestling with a lot of other issues, the attraction hasn't been one-way.'

Her expression was still shrouded in disbelief. 'There's simply no way someone like you could fancy me as much as I fancy them.'

'What do you mean. "someone like me"? A cantankerous ostrich who's floundering in a world he never thought he'd find himself in?'

'See!' she said, as if the fact he'd admitted he was floundering meant she'd been right to put herself down.

'See, what?'

'You're not yourself. You don't know what you're doing. You don't even want your father to meet me.'

He winced. Definitely not one of his finer moments. 'Meet him. He's a Class-A jackass, so maybe it'll be useful for you in figuring out why I am the way I am.'

'Hmm, no. I feel like I just begged for it.'

'The only thing I want you begging for is more of this.'

He tugged her back to him and gave her a kiss that defied the constraints of time.

When they came up for air he said, 'How was that for proof I'm interested?'

'Pretty good.' She scrunched up her nose and grinned up at him. 'I might need a bit more convincing, though.'

He laughed. 'Convincing of what? That I find you completely irresistible?' He gave a low growl, hoping she would translate that into a display of his desire.

'Ooh. Nice start.'

'But...?'

'But you're just...' She patted his chest, then squeezed his biceps and shoulders with a dreamy sigh. 'You're so perfect.'

'And so are you.'

She snorted and gave a little eye-roll.

'Hey. Enough of that.'

He didn't know if it was her ex who'd made her think so poorly of herself, or life in general, but whoever it was had a lot to answer for. He ran his thumb along her lips, pleased when she didn't miss the opportunity to give it a saucy little bite. She was frightened of rejection. He got that. He was terrified of commitment. But wanting her to feel good about herself overrode whatever it was happening between the two of them in the here and now.

'Listen to me.' He swept his hand across her hairline, tracing his fingers along her cheek. 'You're a talented, intelligent, funny, beautiful woman. You do a mean oven glove sock puppet and you seriously rocked in the operating theatre today.' He held up a hand. 'Life isn't perfect. Nor am I. But so far as I can see, your only flaw is your insecurity.'

She pointed at her bare ring finger. 'He didn't exactly leave me feeling good about myself.'

'Well…' Noah looked her straight in the eye. 'He doesn't count any more, does he?'

She gave her head a slow shake.

Noah dropped a few light kisses on her lips, her nose, her brow. 'My darling woman. I don't know if it's a safety blanket you've put on after everything you've been through, but you don't need it. You're amazing. And today you excelled yourself. I was in awe. If anyone has made you think you are anything less than one of the wonders of the world, I'll be more than happy to set them straight.'

He did a couple of silly martial arts moves, gratified to see a smile tease at the corners of her lips.

'Besides,' he added. 'If you think I'm so perfect, why would I lower my perfection standards to slum it?'

'Convenience?'

She was grinning. He ran his hands along her sides and drew her to him for another delicious kiss. 'That wasn't convenience,' he growled. 'That was perfection.'

Her smile shifted into something more sober. 'I guess I told myself that was what I had to believe. That you didn't fancy me. It made the possibility that nothing would happen easier to bear.'

He shook his head confused. 'You're exquisite. Why wouldn't I want you?'

'Uh, apart from the fact I'm not exactly a swimsuit model?' She pressed a finger to his lips to stop his interruption. 'I could hardly pounce on a man grieving for his sister and wrestling with his new identity as guardian to the world's cutest little girls, could I?'

'Oh, I don't know…' he began jokingly, and

then, wanting to honour the honesty she'd offered him, he told her the truth. 'If you've sensed
anything from me, it was only about *me*. I was
scared. I *am* scared. This—' he moved his hand
between the two of them '—whatever this is…
It feels bigger than anything I've ever known,
and I guess I thought ignoring it might be better than screwing it up.'

'That makes two of us.'

He could see she wasn't saying it just to make
him feel better. She was saying it because she
meant it.

'What scares you the most?' he asked.

'That I'll lose myself in you.'

'Is that what happened in your last relationship?'

She nodded. 'I changed my life in a big way
to make that relationship happen, and the idea
of having to start all over again if this goes
wrong—'

'We don't even know what "this" is yet.'

It wasn't exactly a romantic sentiment, but
it needed to be said. She took a moment to let
the thought settle and then flashed him a smile.
'There's no harm in finding out, right?'

He laughed and ran his thumbs along her jaw-
line, pulling her in for a soft kiss. Then another.
And another until he couldn't bear it any more.
He wanted more of her. He wanted skin on skin.

Breath tangling with sighs. The hot, fluid union of his body melding with hers. And by the way she was responding to his touch, she wanted the same thing.

Low moans of approbation reverberated against her throat as he tasted and explored her. He dropped kisses on her jawline, her neck, her throat. His hands enjoyed the purchase they had on those sweet curves between her waist and hips. Anyone who'd made her feel anything other than proud of this body deserved a very stern talking-to.

Her groans became his as she pressed her hips to his, their kisses deepening as she ran her hands over his shoulders and slid them up and around his neck.

'It is so nice to kiss a man who makes me have to go on tiptoe,' she whispered.

'Is that what I've got going for me?' He pulled her in close. 'My height?'

She tipped her head to the side, as if considering the question, and smiled, her lips brushing against his mouth as she said, 'You might have one or two other assets I wouldn't mind having access to.'

The words dropped a firebomb directly into his erogenous zones. His erection pulsed with desire. The naughty smile on her lips showed she'd felt it and liked knowing she was the reason he was hard.

Where the hell had this version of Rebecca risen from? Talk about phoenix from the ashes.

'Want to get out of here?' he asked.

'No,' she said. 'I just want you.'

CHAPTER TWELVE

REBECCA TRACED HER fingers round the neckline of Noah's scrubs feeling like an emboldened goddess. Aphrodite? Maybe. Whichever one was filled to the brim with pent-up lust.

As she tugged him in for the most scorching kiss she'd ever stolen from a man she curled her fingers tight around the vee of the cotton fabric—then ripped it.

To their mutual astonishment the fabric tore right in half—just as she'd hoped. A minor miracle if ever there was one. Not as miraculous as being locked in an examination room snogging the man of her dreams, but…*mmm*…her brain turned to mush as he tugged her in for another kiss.

When he pulled back, she hovered her hands over his golden skin. 'Can I?' she asked.

'I'd be very upset if you didn't.' He swallowed, his Adam's apple all but spelling out the question he wasn't asking: Who the hell had stolen Rebecca and replaced her with this sex kitten?

It was a good question. One she didn't have the answer to. And frankly she didn't much care. She liked this version of herself. She was sassy.

She scraped her nails across the span of Noah's shoulders, shifting the rest of the thick cotton out of the way. 'We won't be needing that,' she said as it slid to the ground.

Noah murmured something she didn't quite catch, but she caught the gist of it. *Please don't stop.*

So she carried on.

She shamelessly admired his bare chest and then, pushing him back across the room so that he was forced to hoist himself up onto the counter, she grinned. 'There…' She ran the tip of one of her nails around the dark areola of his nipple, instantly making it go hard. 'Just the perfect height to do this.' She swept her tongue round the same nipple, skidding her fingers over the other one until it, too, went hard.

'Who even *are* you?' he breathed through a moan as she pressed her hand onto his erection.

'I'm your gift from the universe.' She smiled, then ran her fingertips along his six-pack, thrilling in the response of his musculature as she touched him.

Rebecca felt, for the very first time, as if her body, mind and spirit were at one with themselves. But she realised with startling clarity that she wasn't different. She was finally herself. And she liked who she was. This version of her would never undress in the dark and run to hide under the covers so her lover wouldn't see her body, as she had with her ex. This one would wear high heels when she wanted. This one would never turn crimson in shame because of her Rubenesque curves. This one enjoyed being in Noah's arms. She felt sensual and desired. Powerful. It was a delicious elixir like the fabled milk and honey…and she was ready to drink from its cup.

She pinched the fabric waist tie of Noah's scrubs between two of her fingers and tugged as she met his eyes. 'I don't think we'll be needing these either.'

Noah's eyes blinked wide. A flicker of fear ran through her that she'd taken this whole emboldened-like-a-goddess thing a step too far, but… *Hmm*. What was that pressing against her thigh? She smiled as he pulled her in closer. If the strength of his erection was anything to go by, he liked it.

'Let's even the playing field, shall we?'

He teased his fingers beneath the hem of her scrubs top. She hadn't bothered putting on a bra, and just the idea of his fingers reaching her breasts sent a surge of heat through her.

Noah took his time, shifting the cotton away with the backs of his hands as his fingertips whispered along her skin with tantalising slowness. He teased goosebumps out of the delicate indentations at her waist...the soft skin along her sides. She arched towards him as his fingers neared her breasts. As if sensing she wanted nothing more than to feel his skin against hers, he whipped her top up and over her head, slipped off the countertop, pulled her to him.

The effect on her body was instantaneous. As if her bones had turned to rubber and heated fistfuls of glitter had been released into her nervous system. He slid his hands to her bum, and before she could figure out what he was doing he'd lifted her up and round and placed her on the counter, where he'd just been.

A richly satisfied look flickered through his eyes as he repeated her phrase. 'Ah...just the perfect height to do this.'

He cupped one of her breasts with his hand and, while lightly stroking the other with the backs of his fingers, began to lazily twirl his tongue round her nipple. Again, she arched towards him, enjoying the pleasure he was openly taking in increasing her desire. She'd not experienced this before. An equality of passion. Desire to please. Two equals with one mutual interest at heart. To bring the other person joy.

Beneath Noah's caresses, his tongue, his mouth, her breasts felt plump and full. Not that they'd ever been tiny, but she felt no shame in the luxurious opulence of them now. His physique was such that she felt feminine in his arms. Delicate from the way he touched her. And positively primal when he slid her scrubs bottoms off her legs and ran his hands up along between her thighs until he reached the triangle between her legs, slipping first one, then two fingers into her to dizzying effect.

Not having a shirt to grab hold of any more, she ran her fingers through his soft black hair, curling them into small fistfuls of the silky ebony depths. When his touch threatened to overwhelm her, she tugged him away from her, her voice shaking as she said, 'I want you. Now.'

He didn't need any more encouragement. What followed was fast and delicious. Two voracious appetites sating themselves…pleasuring each other's body.

Mercifully, they'd tumbled into a room that had an ample supply of protection. She would've taken her time sheathing him, but the pulsing between her legs demanded urgent action.

He turned her so that her back was to him. The warmth from his chest radiated through her.

Her breath hitched as his erection teased apart her legs. Her core turned molten as, once again, his fingers slipped through her soft curls to her clitoris. Her heart lurched around her ribcage... her body was physically aching with unfulfilled desire until she all but begged him to enter her.

Though she hadn't ever had sex this way before—her ex had been quite a traditionalist when it came to those things: bed, covers, one of two positions and this wasn't one of them— she already knew she liked it.

Noah spread his hands along the sides of her waist and, after a few gentle, teasing entrances, slid his full length into her. His hands swept up her sides and cupped her breasts as she pushed back into him, wriggling her bum until the very tip of his erection hit the magic spot that lit her up like the Eiffel Tower. They groaned in tandem, and then an organic rhythm took hold of them as they began to move.

They were beyond language now. Beyond instructions. Instinct took over in a way she'd never imagined possible. This was the type of magic she'd expect between two seasoned lovers. Not lust-filled, half-exhausted, adrenaline-fuelled surgeons so far out of their depth neither of them could see beyond today, let along the next month or year.

And yet...none of it mattered. Not the fear, the

fatigue, the future. Because for the first time in her life she was living in the moment. Not for a spreadsheet, not for a deadline. She was living for the here and now with Noah. For his touch. His deep thrust and his rich groans of desire. Noah *knew* her. Her body. Her rhythms. The perfect place to hold her hips as he increased the shared rhythm building between their bodies.

All at once she felt a sea change in their movements. As if they had literally become one. Noah's intense, organic thrusts came more intuitively, matching the undulations of her hips. Intellectually, she knew they were both moving faster, more urgently, but something in her brain was processing the pulsing of their bodies as a sybaritic decadence. As if each thrust was unveiling another pleasure zone deep within her. Until wave after wave of heat swept through her and Noah clasped her to him, his hips trying and failing to contain the fundamental thrusts his body was succumbing to as they reached their climaxes in tandem.

As the waves of pleasure eased, leaving her body humming with pleasure, Rebecca felt an extraordinary combination of drained and elated. As if she were literally floating on air. Noah turned her round, his body warm with exertion, and pulled her to him. He dropped a light kiss on her lips, then rested his chin on her head as they wrapped their arms around one another and allowed their breathing to settle.

After a few moments of silence, Rebecca pulled back and smiled up at him. 'Did you want to get back to the girls?'

He tugged his discarded scrubs from the floor and pulled his mobile phone out of the pocket and checked for messages.

'Looks like they went to sleep after a double dose of story time.'

He scanned her, as if reliving the sex they'd just shared. If she'd thought she might be able to head off to sleep, she'd been wrong.

'Fancy a midnight snack?'

'Absolutely.' She gave him a cheeky grin. 'How about we have it at my villa, just in case we make any noise?'

He play-growled his approval and pulled her in for another groan-inducing kiss. Which, of course, made them laugh. It felt so good to do this. To laugh. To feel as if she belonged in someone's arms.

They both pulled on their scrubs and gave the room a quick tidy, dissolving into giggles when they examined the ripped remains of Noah's top.

'I think I'm going to have to make a donation to the clinic for destroying clinic property.' Rebecca laughed.

Noah held up the remains of his top and then

gave her a look that suggested he hoped this wouldn't be the first and only time she ripped his clothes off. 'What do you say we open a tab?'

The second time they made love, it was as gentle as the breeze undulating the mosquito netting around Rebecca's four-poster bed. They had all the shuttered windows wide open to the night sky. Their movements fell naturally in sync with the sound of the distant waves, lulling them into a beautiful organic place where their bodies might as well have been filled with phosphorescence.

Getting to touch and kiss Noah's body in this way felt luxurious. Even more so to have him explore her body in the same way. While there was no chance she would've traded in that frantic, voracious lovemaking back at the clinic, this felt less like getting access to an entire chocolate cake for one minute and more like being offered an all-day brunch with an open champagne bar.

It felt new to indulge in touching and being touched—to put life and all its craziness on hold while they explored one another's bodies as if they had all the time in the world. No. It didn't just feel good. It felt right.

When they'd reached an all-consuming climax, luxuriating in the waves of pleasure they'd unleashed in the other's body, they fell asleep in one another's arms, spent from a day that had seen them at both extremes.

Rebecca felt the sun on her face before she opened her eyes. She yawned and stretched like a cat, her eyes popping wide open when she realised Noah had gone.

Her blood ran cold.

It was the one thought she hadn't allowed herself. The one fear.

That Noah would regret what had happened between them.

She was about to go into a tailspin of panic—and then her eyes lit on the clock.

Gah!

Lovers' remorse was one thing, but being late for work when the man she'd bared her soul to was her boss was an entirely different affair.

She flew into the shower and tugged on a pair of scrubs.

She was stuffing her hair into a topknot as she came down the stairs from her bedroom, wishing she had time to run across the street for one of the fruit drinks she'd become addicted to—and, of course, a coffee—when she saw a steaming cup of takeaway coffee sitting next to a smoothie on the kitchen counter, along with a note.

She picked it up, hands shaking with nerves.

Before she'd read anything more than her name, she closed her eyes against the neat script.

Please, please, please don't let it be a good-bye.

Having wild, spontaneous sex, then making slow, mesmeric love was so far outside her experience she barely recognised the body she was walking around in, let alone the woman who'd ravished Noah last night. She had investigated his body as if he was a sexy crime scene. Explored each millimetre of his body. The tattoos, the curves, the taut musculature...

But it wasn't just his body she'd fallen head over heels for—because that was what she'd done. It wasn't a crush. It wasn't lust. It wasn't a holiday romance. She'd taken a step off a cliff she'd never thought she'd step off again and done the unimaginable. She'd fallen in love with Noah Cameron, knowing his was a heart she'd never be able to call her own.

She forced herself to open her eyes, steeling her heart for the inevitable.

Wanted to take the girls to school. See you at the clinic. I think we need to talk before they get home.

All the insecurities she'd thought she'd dealt with crashed in on her like a tsunami.

Her professional goals.

Her desire for a family.

Her desire to be loved *for* her quirks, not despite them.

None of it was enough.

Noah hadn't spelled it out because he hadn't needed to.

A 'talk' before the girls came home meant only one thing. Noah wanted to shut down what had happened between them before the girls got attached.

The coffee was a nice touch. Considerate. It showed he was trying to be respectful of her feelings. But Rebecca knew now that a coffee and a smoothie had never been the endgame. Love had.

She clutched her arms round her stomach, doubling over on herself. What was it about her that made men walk away? The pain was unimaginable. She felt it on a cellular level. Straight through to her essence.

Because it wasn't just Noah rejecting her—it was history repeating itself. Once again Rebecca had chosen a man who didn't want to be 'pinned down'. Not by her, anyway.

After she and her ex had done everything by the book, literally—they'd even had a planner detailing how their futures would pan out—she'd taken her broken heart and tried to heal it by throwing it in the polar opposite direction. She'd harnessed her trust, her compassion, her willingness to let the universe do its work on her behalf, and had still been proved to have the instincts of a moth to a flame.

She couldn't face another rejection. Not from Noah. Not after opening her heart up to him the way she had.

The pain twisted in on itself. She couldn't even blame him. The girls had to come first for him. She was free to pick up her life and relocate it wherever she wanted—but he didn't have the same luxury.

There was only one solution for it. She'd have to end things so he didn't have to bear the extra burden of guilt.

She grabbed her backpack and set off for the clinic, grateful to her grapefruit shower gel for taking Noah's scent away from her skin. It would have been one reminder too many of what she was letting go.

She forced herself to become the sensible, fact-based woman she'd been when she'd flown into Bali. The one who honoured science and statistics and empirical evidence. The one who devoted her life to medicine. She had that to thank him for. Giving her a job that had reminded her where her energies were best spent: on other people's children.

Perhaps that was what last night had really been. A thank-you shag for reminding her of her true passion: paediatric surgery.

The emotion of yesterday's intense surgeries had clearly made them lose perspective on life. They'd lost and saved lives and, although they were trained to maintain a clinical distance— especially in the operating theatre—occasionally the human drama of a case crept into their bones and made itself heard. Yesterday had been one of those occasions.

It must've been particularly hard going for Noah, who knew exactly what it felt like to think everything was perfectly fine one minute and then, with just one poorly driven vehicle, have everything change. She could've kicked herself for not taking that into account last night. Of *course* he'd been feeling vulnerable. And she'd *launched* herself at him.

Shame deepened her misery.

How could she have been so blind? So insensitive?

Of course last night had been nothing more than a fluke. A one-off to dilute the painful memories that must surely have been at play when he'd pulled her into his arms.

She'd never been his endgame.

He had children to look after. Enormous decisions to make. Like whether or not he'd move back to Australia, for example. Or keep the clinic a going concern. They were just the tip of an enormous iceberg's worth of decisions. There was no chance a woman trying to find her 'true self' after being epically dumped registered anywhere but in the fathomless icy depths of his To Do list.

But he treated you like a queen. He made you feel beautiful.

It was true. He had. She'd never felt more desired. And that should be what she took away from this. Not sorrow.

He'd done nothing to make her feel horrible about herself. This was a holiday romance. Nothing more. Nothing less. Nothing to feel ashamed about. Not yet anyway.

All of which made now the perfect time to draw a line under it all and move on.

In an emotional about-face her serenity coach would've applauded, Rebecca chucked out the filter of self-pity she'd been using and vowed to do the right thing by Noah.

She would take the decision-making out of his hands and make it crystal-clear that the night had been a one-off. She would shoulder the blame for their hedonistic lovemaking sessions. The moans, the groans, the ripped shirt. She'd taken advantage of him at a time when they'd both been vulnerable.

He'd openly told her he was floundering. That he was struggling to make decisions. Well, this was one decision he wouldn't have to make.

Would her heart crack in two as she stepped back into the friend zone? *Definitely.* But their friendship had empowered her. Reminded her that she was a woman with her own mind, her own profession, her own voice.

It was time she used all of them.

She took a sip of the coffee and sighed. *So good.*

Despite her determination to see her decision through, prickles of sadness teased at the back of her throat. Bringing her coffee and inviting her to lunch to tell her he just wasn't that into her was gentlemanly. Miles better than her ex's lack of consideration. Leaving his laptop on the kitchen table, open to his girlfriend's pregnancy scans, had been a fairly traumatic way of finding out her intended had other intentions.

If Noah was to be her solitary rebound experience she should thank heaven above that it had been as celestial as it had. How could she regret learning just how sublime lovemaking could be? It had never been like that with her ex, or anyone before him. It had set a whole new bar. One she would insist upon in any future lovers.

When she arrived at the clinic she checked in with the charge nurse, who gave her an update on the infant and the two-year-old boy. They were both still in the clinic's cobbled-together version of an intensive care unit, and would be transferred to the main hospital with its better staffed unit later this afternoon, as soon as the building got its all-clear. Noah was down there now.

'Great!' Rebecca chirped. 'Grand.'

More time to come up with the perfect way to release him from any commitment he might feel he owed her.

Two cases of Bali Belly, one monkey bite that hadn't broken the skin and three rather savage coral cuts later, Rebecca looked up at the sound of a knock on the door to the office she'd been using to make notes.

Noah.

All her vows to be a brand-new version of herself evaporated.

How could they not?

He was all golden-skinned and ebony-haired. Blue-black eyes glittering like the night sky. His tattoos, each of which she'd run her tongue along, were peeking out from beneath the sleeves of his black scrubs.

Her eyes darted to the door.

He saw the move.

'Don't worry,' he said, pushing it even wider open. 'You're safe.'

Her face must've looked stricken, because his virtually mirrored hers when their eyes met.

They both spoke at once, their hurried apologies tumbling over each other.

'Sorry. I—I meant I probably shouldn't have instigated—' he began.

'I should be the one assuring you that you're safe with—' she said.

They both pulled themselves up short. Their eyes caught and locked, each of them actively searching the other's gaze for answers.

Noah looked different today. Softer. More approachable. Surely it couldn't be because he was falling for her the same way she had fallen for him?

Why did you dump the man of your dreams?

Because you knew it was the right thing to do.

'We should probably draw a line under what happened last night,' she said.

His expression remained neutral, but something flared in his eyes that made it clear he had not seen that coming. Not from her, anyway.

'Fair enough.' He nodded, and then, as if closing the door on that very brief, incredibly perfect chapter in their lives, said in a voice almost bereft of emotion, 'The girls have to be my priority.'

Tears stung at the back of her throat. He'd tried to disguise it, but she heard the regret in his voice. So she said the only thing she could. 'Of course they do.'

'They woke up last night and couldn't find me.'

The information pierced through what she now realised was a gossamer-thin layer of confidence. The tears she'd been holding back skidded down her cheeks. 'I'm so sorry. Are they all right?'

'They are now.'

She heard what he was saying. Now that he'd reassured them he would always be there for them. Exclusively. As he should be. They'd all experienced too much loss to endure any moments of unnecessary pain. Of course she wanted Noah. But not at the expense of the girls' happiness and security.

'I'm so sorry. I didn't know.'

'And yet you pipped me to the post.' He tipped his finger towards her, then to himself, before curling his hand into a fist. 'Calling an end to this.'

'I—I just thought, as you've got so much on your plate, you don't need extra complications.'

'Is that how you see what's been developing between us? As a complication?'

'Not for me...' She floundered, suddenly panicked that she'd read the situation incorrectly. 'I think you're amazing. I have from the moment I very first saw you. But…yesterday was intense. Before we…' She threw her hands up in the air. 'When you weren't there this morning, I guess I thought I was one extra thing on your list of things to do that you didn't need to worry about. There's a lot I need to sort out in my life too. You shouldn't have to deal with that as well.'

Noah seemed to let the comment sink in. Then, to her sorrow, she watched as he morphed back into the man she'd first met a few weeks ago. The one who kept his emotions in check. Whose smiles were rare. The one whose thoughts were impossible to read.

'Fair enough,' he said, as if she'd casually mentioned she was becoming a vegetarian after having a bad steak. 'Probably just as well. My dad's arriving today, and the girls and I are out to dinner with him tonight, so…'

He didn't need to finish the sentence.

As you weren't invited anyway, it's best not to muddy the waters more than we already have.

'Okay.'

She wove her fingers together, too aware that what she really wanted to do was to wrap her arms around him. Hug him. Kiss him. Ask him to sit down and talk, see if there wasn't some way they could work this out. But she knew in her heart he had to do what he thought best. Just because he'd given her a three-month contract, several delicious weeks of frisson and one night of bliss, it didn't mean he owed her a happily-ever-after. This wasn't real life for either of them. It was time to face reality and move on.

She put on what she hoped was a friendly smile and asked, 'Would it be best if I left now? Or would you like me to see out the last few weeks of my contract?'

CHAPTER THIRTEEN

NOAH FELT AWFUL. He'd never experienced the sensation of being utterly torn in two, but something was telling him this was exactly what it felt like.

'The staff would be delighted if you stayed. I know the girls would like it, too. As you know, they're not good with abrupt departures.'

A fresh crop of tears glistened in her eyes. She didn't say anything, but he could see the question in her eyes. The one he wasn't answering. What did he want?

Of course he wanted her to stay. But it would only make her inevitable departure more difficult.

Last night he'd felt connected to Rebecca in a way he'd never experienced before. They were on a professional par. She was amazing with the girls. And, more importantly, she was balm to his soul. She made him want to be a better man.

For the first time in his life he'd had those

three precious words floating on the tip of his tongue all night long. He was grateful now he hadn't said them. How could he have told her he loved her and then explained a handful of hours later that he wasn't strong enough to both love Rebecca *and* do what was best for the girls? Falling on the 'men aren't multi-taskers' stereotype simply wasn't good enough.

He dug into his pocket and handed her a fresh handkerchief.

She took it, but refused to meet his eyes.

He wanted to tell her he'd woken up *happy.* That wasn't something that had come prepacked in his toolbox. Straight-up happiness. And, goddammit, he'd woken up at *peace.* For the first time ever he had been genuinely looking forward to seeing his father, so he could introduce him to the woman he hoped would be in his life…well, for ever.

He'd never introduced his father to anyone. There'd never been any point. And today there wasn't either. Because the time had finally come for him to start making those difficult decisions about the girls, the clinic, and all their futures. Decisions he'd have to make independent of Rebecca. Decisions he knew his father would've made the day Indah died.

'What do *you* want, Noah?' Rebecca pressed.

He wanted her. But he couldn't have her. Not

now. Not like this. Not when he couldn't give her everything she deserved.

He took the British coin out of his pocket, gave the proud warrior a look, then placed it on the desk between them. 'It's your life, Rebecca. So this should be your call.'

And then he walked away.

She called out after him, but he kept walking. He had a clinic to run. News to break to the girls. A father's disappointment to shoulder. Might as well lose himself in a few hours' work, first.

A few long-legged strides later he was in front of the charge nurse. He nodded at the patient board. 'Right. Where do I start?'

A few hours later, with not enough patients to wipe what had happened from his brain, Noah was buttoning up a fresh shirt when Isla and Ruby knocked on his door.

'Hey, girls, come on in.'

He'd already broken the news that Rebecca wouldn't be joining them later and, as expected, it hadn't gone down a storm. He hadn't told them the real reason, of course. He'd said she had to work late and she was sorry she wouldn't be making it.

They'd been gutted. He knew they loved him, but they lit up whenever Rebecca was about. She had that effect on kids. She was a natural hugger. Loved board games. Knew when to tease, when to back off. She was good with them. She made him a better parent to them, and it was killing him that it couldn't continue.

Because as much as she improved him she also threw him off balance. And that simply wasn't an option. Especially with everything they'd gone through.

Was this how he'd always handled things? Waiting for the right place? The right time? Only to realise there never was one?

He silently cursed himself as the girls wrapped their arms round his waist. He'd known how he felt about Rebecca from the first day he'd met her. And for some idiot reason he'd thought keeping those feelings to himself had been the smart thing to do.

No wonder she wanted out. Who wanted a man who couldn't make a decision and stick to it? One who fell head over heels in love only to pull the plug.

His cousin was right. He was a structured, routine-orientated guy, who excelled in the workplace. And that was it. It was time to head back to Australia and give the girls a solid foundation for their futures. Fancy schools. Elite country clubs. A stay-at-home mum... Well... They'd have whatever nanny his cousin had chosen, anyway. Someone far better qualified to give these girls the TLC they deserved.

'Uncle Noah?' Ruby was giving him one of her most soulful, pleading looks.

'Yes, darlin'?'

'Do you think if we made Rebecca a carrot cake she would come to supper with us tonight?'

Noah swept his hand across Ruby's hair and gave Isla's shoulder a squeeze. 'I don't think we have time, love. Your granddad is due to meet us at the restaurant in half an hour.'

'Maybe we should leave her a note to tell her where we are?' Isla's little brow crinkled with concern. 'Just in case she finishes in time?'

Noah squatted down so he was at the girls' eye level, using the pads of his thumbs to smooth the furrows away. 'I'm sure she would've joined us if she could. She's got a lot of patients to see today.'

'Maybe they'll all feel better soon and she'll be hungry.' Isla threw a look at Ruby, who nodded. They'd obviously been discussing this. 'We should probably tell her.'

He was going to say no, but their little faces were so filled with hope he thought *Why not?*

After they'd spoken this afternoon she hadn't stropped off to pack her bags and leave. She'd made it clear to the charge nurse, who'd passed on the news to him, that she was going to see through the three-month commitment she'd made. The last thing she'd do was begrudge the girls a hug and a kiss goodbye.

'She's with her patients right now, but why don't you make her a card or a drawing? She'd like that.'

The girls oohed and told him that was a good idea. 'Do you want to make her one, too?'

He smiled and shook his head. The only thing he wanted to do right now was to ask Rebecca to stay. But he'd be asking her to live her life in limbo. To maybe live in Bali. Maybe live in Sydney. Definitely give up her life in England, the way his own mother had given up her life here to follow a man. It hadn't worked out well for his mother. And he simply couldn't abide the thought of anything similar happening to Rebecca. Which was why the sensible decision to end things now had to be the path they chose.

'Uncle Noah, you look sad,' Ruby said. 'Do you wish Rebecca was coming, too?'

'Yeah,' he admitted. 'I do. But she can't, so it's just going to be the three of us.'

The girls threw their arms around his neck and squeezed. This would work. The three of them. There was enough love here to make whatever path they chose the right one. Wasn't there?

'Well, go on, then,' he said to the girls, shooing them out of his room with a semi-stern warning that they had ten minutes.

The girls ran off to find their crayons to draw Rebecca a card. Time Noah spent glaring at his own reflection. He briefly considered cutting off his hair. A classic 'man in crisis' move. But he knew if he did his father would make some jibe or another. *Finally seen the light and become a real man, have you son?* So he left it. Besides, he'd used Rebecca's shampoo that morning and, as stupid and romantic as it was, he liked having that essence of her with him. However fleeting.

After the girls had run across to her villa and delivered the card, Noah bundled them into the Jeep to meet his father. Just a few more hours to grit his teeth through before he could go home and figure out how the hell he was going to confront the rest of his life.

CHAPTER FOURTEEN

'HERE'S YOUR VALET parking slip, Dr Cameron.'

'Thank you.'

'Ooh,' said Isla as she slipped her hand into his after handing her light sweater to the cloakroom girl. 'Fancy.'

'Sure is,' Noah said.

It always was if his father had chosen it. For as long as he could remember, his father had only dined in fancy Michelin-starred restaurants. 'Research', he called it. But Noah knew what it really was. Posing.

Though his father rarely mentioned it, he came from a humble background. Downright poor, if they were going to be truthful. He'd been a jobbing farm labourer's son. His father had picked up contract work on vast estates owned by barely there owners. People so rich they could helicopter in from the city to check up on their staff in between jaunts to holiday hotspots.

Being one of the have-nots had fuelled Noah's

father to become the driven, highly successful businessman he was today. At last count he'd owned twenty A-list resorts, tactically dotted around the globe.

Noah scanned the restaurant, instinctively looking for the chef's table—the only place his father would sit. Ah. There he was, looking every bit the patriarch, lording it over the rest of the diners. Shock of white hair. Piercing blue eyes. The same steely build. From a distance, anyway.

He forced himself to remember that his dad was on his own again, and very possibly would be feeling just the slightest bit vulnerable. Then again...this was his dad they were talking about. Probably not.

Noah steered the girls across the room towards their grandfather, willing the meal to be à la carte rather than one of those endless chef's menus. Whatever his father had to say, he could say over the appetisers.

'Hello, Noah.' His bright blue eyes made a quick scan of his son, and in a rare turn of events he kept his observations to himself.

'Father,' Noah replied in a stiff, formal voice he only used for—well, his father.

Though they didn't maintain eye contact for long, for a fraction of a second Noah thought he saw a frailty he'd never noted in his father before. Old age? His father was a fairly robust sixty-five, so he doubted that.

Loneliness?

The word popped into his head and stuck. Newly single. Deceased daughter. Estranged son. Maybe his instinct to be concerned had been the right one.

'Girls.' His father gave each of the girls a nod rather than pulling them into his arms.

They looked up at him, confused. Noah gave both girls a quick tight hug before pointing them towards chairs, realising as he did so that it was a gesture he might not have done before meeting Rebecca. He zipped up the memory and set it aside. Tonight wasn't the night to rehash his failings.

As they got themselves settled, Noah asked the waiter for some soft drinks for the girls and a large bottle of water for himself.

'I've ordered a rather delightful Chablis,' his father cut in.

The last thing he and his father needed to maintain a civilised conversation was alcohol. 'Thanks, Dad. I'm driving. Water's fine.'

His father drew in a sharp breath, presumably to remind Noah that fine food was best enjoyed with fine wine, when his eyes lit on someone at the entrance to the restaurant. Noah's back was to the door, but the girls followed their grandfather's eyeline, their dark eyes widening as they hit the entrance.

'Rebecca!' the girls squealed in tandem, jumping down from their chairs and racing across the restaurant floor to hug her.

Noah turned, his lungs taking a hit as he saw her.

She was beautiful any day of the week, but tonight she looked out of this world.

She'd left her hair loose, allowing it to flow over her shoulders in flame-coloured pre-Raphaelite waves. She was wearing an aqua-blue dress that draped over one shoulder, leaving the other bare. The silky fabric skidded over her curves and fluttered in her wake as she walked towards them, her feet tucked into delicate heels the colour of the sea.

She met Noah's gaze head-on, with a smile and a proud confidence that suited her. 'Sorry I'm late. I hope the invitation still stands.'

'What are you doing here?' he asked quietly.

'Friends don't let friends dine with estranged fathers alone.'

Before he could respond, she handed him the card the girls had drawn for her.

It showed two little girls holding hands with two adults. One with dark hair and dark blue eyes and one with bright red hair and green eyes. There were hearts drawn all around the family.

Underneath the drawing, written in childlike handwriting were the words *Family = Love*.

Noah's father, characteristically using his arsenal of charm, rose from his chair and signalled to a waiter to bring a chair for Rebecca. 'We can't deny a beautiful woman like this a place at our table—can we, Noah?' He pointedly looked to his son for an explanation.

'This is Rebecca,' Noah began, instantly floundering when it came to deciding how to describe her.

'She's Uncle Noah's girlfriend,' Ruby said.

Noah's heart froze in place.

Rebecca's eyes flicked between Ruby's and Isla's. She smiled, and then, in a move he wasn't expecting, crossed her fingers and gave a hopeful little shrug.

Noah's eyes snapped to hers, and in that instant he saw what he should've seen back when they were at the clinic. She loved him, too.

His heart crashed against his ribcage, over and over, drumming out clamorous thumps of gratitude, relief and wonder.

But if she loved him why had she cut things short?

His mind flashed back to the note he'd written.

We need to talk.

He'd meant he'd wanted to talk to her about his father. Because if there was one thing in the world Noah could predict it was that his father only visited when he had plans, and Noah had wanted the two of them to be braced for it, armed with a plan of their own. A united front.

We need to talk.

In a sudden flash of understanding, he realised Rebecca had thought he'd given her the beginnings of a *Dear John* letter.

So of course she'd called it quits. She'd been treated horrifically by her ex and having been so brave, so bold, as to open up her heart to *him*, the last thing she was going to do was let him crush it under his foot like dirt. Or, from another angle, she'd done what she'd thought best. Made a complicated situation simpler. She knew he was struggling. She'd been trying to help.

'Before you sit...' Her expression remained unchanged, but her eyes snapped to his, flaring when they met and meshed. How the hell could he have walked away from her...? It was a mistake he was never going to make again. 'I just want to ask you a couple of things about a patient, if you don't mind.'

'Not at all.' Her smile remained an enchanting

combination of soft and strong. As if she'd found her happy place and nothing would take it away.

She gave the girls a quick kiss on the tops of their heads and somehow bewitched his father into asking the waiter for colouring pencils, to help him explain to the girls what all the fancy dishes were.

They walked out into the garden at the back of the restaurant. There were palm trees wrapped with swirls of fairy lights. A koi pond with a bridge over it beckoned a few metres away from the building.

He held his hand out to guide her there.

'I hope I haven't overstepped,' she said before he could say anything. 'I was thinking if you and your father needed some alone time the girls and I could leave early. But if I've read the situation incorrectly again...' She winced. 'Oh, God. I have, haven't I? I'm sorry. I—'

He held up his hand, then dragged it through his hair before looking her in the eye. 'I'm the one who owes you an apology.'

She took one of his hands in hers, weaving her fingers through his as she shook her head. She lifted her gaze to meet his. 'I—I think I might have jumped the gun this morning.'

'I think we *both* might have jumped the gun this morning.'

'The note,' she said. 'The one you wrote—'

'It was meant to be the *beginning* of something,' Noah explained. 'Not the end.'

Her cheeks pinkened as she gave him a sheepish smile. 'That occurred to me later. Much later.' She flicked her eyes towards the restaurant. 'As you can see, I still have insecurities.'

'Hey...' He reached out to give her arm a squeeze. 'All this is new to both of us. We're bound to misunderstand one another from time to time. But let me be clear: I am very happy that our friendship has developed into something more...' He selected the word carefully, pressing his hands to his heart as he said it. 'Meaningful.'

She held up the card the girls had drawn for her. 'Before today I didn't think crayon drawings were powerful, but...but this one showed me something I needed to be reminded of.'

'What's that?'

'That real love—true love—is strong. It's about being a friend, more than a lover. It endures misunderstandings. It stands up against hurt and pain and it doesn't crumble at the first mishap.' She looked down at her hands, then back up at him. 'I love you, Noah. I wanted to tell you that this morning. But even thinking that you might not love me back—'

He didn't leave her hanging this time. 'I do, my darling. My beautiful, beautiful gift from the universe.' They laughed and, as the sound sighed away, Noah continued. 'I love you, Rebecca Stone. Something I was too thick-headed to realise until you were strong enough to walk away from me.'

'Strong?' She grimaced. 'I think that was cowardice at work.'

He shook his head. 'No. It was strong to let me know you wanted to be loved the way you deserve to be loved. Wholly. With commitment and openness.'

Rebecca pressed a hand to his heart, letting the gesture do the talking for her. Their lives would be woven together now. Stronger because they were two.

'You said you wanted to talk to me about your dad?'

He grimaced as he tipped his head towards the dining room. 'I'm fairly certain he's going to offer to buy the clinic back from me. Turn it back into a hotel so the girls and I can move to Sydney "unencumbered."'

Rebecca paled, her face frozen in alarm. 'Is that what you want?'

'It's what I thought I wanted when I first flew out here, but…' He pulled her in closer to him. 'Then I met you.'

Her lips tipped into a smile. 'What does your meeting me have to do with the clinic?'

'The clinic was set up to be a legacy to my

mother and her commitment to us. But if I'm being honest it never would have become anything if my sister hadn't put the plan into action.'

'You paid for everything!' Rebecca protested.

He shrugged the fact away. 'There are loads of people I could have gone to to be donors.'

'Like your father?'

'Like my father.'

'But you didn't want his money?'

Noah shook his head. 'No.' He clenched his jaw tight before admitting, 'It was his approval I was after.'

Rebecca closed her eyes, and when she opened them they glistened with un-spilt emotion.

Noah leant forward and gave her a soft kiss. 'I don't need it any more,' he said, adding, 'Someone very wise suggested I open my eyes to what the universe is offering, and it turns out it's giving me closure on that part of my life.'

'Noah… That's wonderful.'

'And that's why I wanted to talk to you. With closure comes new beginnings. And I'm wondering if you'd like to make a new beginning here, with me and the girls?'

Rebecca's eyes began to rapid blink. 'In Bali?'

He nodded. 'Yup.'

'What about your life back in Sydney?'

'It's not much of a life, to be honest. I've a couple of ideas I can run past the director about

setting up an adjunct orthopaedic clinic here...
but I'd feel a lot better working it out together
with you, if you're willing.'

Her smile turned mischievous. 'Are you saying you want to work it out with your *girlfriend*?'

'If you're happy to be my girlfriend.' The line
was cheesy, but at this exact moment he didn't
care. He felt like a lovestruck teen. Rebecca was
the woman he wanted. To work with, to play
with, to love.

'How's this for an answer?' she asked, and
went up on tiptoe to give him a long, slow, delicious kiss.

As coolly as he could manage, he whispered
against her lips, 'That'll do. For now.' He swept
his hands along her hips, then gave her bum a
cheeky squeeze. 'We'd probably better get in
there and rescue the girls.'

'Let's do that,' she agreed.

And after another sweeter than honey kiss,
hand in hand, they went into the restaurant to
face their future as a couple.

CHAPTER FIFTEEN

A FEW DAYS LATER, Noah finished tucking the girls in, then went back downstairs, where his father was laughing at some anecdote Rebecca was telling him about her grandmother.

'So the old bird's grown some new wings?' His father guffawed, instantly lowering his voice when he saw Noah—a reminder that there were two little girls trying to go to sleep upstairs.

Noah shook his head, astonished at the dozens of tiny little miracles that had materialised since he'd opened his heart to Rebecca. Wrapping his father round her little finger for one.

His father hadn't unveiled a grand plan, in the end. They'd simply done what his family had never done. Enjoyed a meal together. Laughed. Caught up on general news. Shared bites of their genuinely delicious food. It had felt both normal and extraordinary. And it continued to catch him out as each day passed.

Rebecca looked up, her smile brightening as she caught Noah's eye. 'Everything all right?'

Noah nodded and joined Rebecca on the sofa across from his father. 'Apart from the girls asking if they can have truffled risotto for their lunch tomorrow, everything's grand.'

He gave his father a begrudging smile. 'Thanks for yet another meal out, Dad. It was delicious.'

His father went through a strange throat-clearing exercise, and Noah was just about to get up and give him a thump on the back when he realised his dad was fighting back a swell of emotion.

He felt Rebecca's hand slip into his and give it a squeeze before she rose and got his father some water. There really was strength in numbers. Especially if that number was two.

'Here you are, Mr Cameron.'

'Reggie.'

The instruction was a plea. Devoid of his father's usual put-on charm and panache. He really wanted Rebecca to treat him like family.

Noah crossed to him. 'Are you all right, Dad?' They both knew he wasn't asking about his throat.

'Yes, son.' His father leant forward, elbows on knees, and after a few moments said, 'I've received a few wake-up calls these past few months.'

'Oh?'

'It's not my health. That's fine.'

The relief in Noah's chest caught him by surprise. He'd certainly never wished his father ill, but the fact he wasn't unwell was an enormous relief. 'Good. Good...'

'It's more I think it's time I smelt the roses a bit. Do you hear what I'm saying?'

'I think you'd better spell it out.'

His dad glanced across at Rebecca. 'You're happy for Rebecca to hear my plan?'

Noah nodded. 'She's a smart woman. I look to her for advice.' Though he kept his eyes on his father, he felt the warmth of Rebecca's smile.

'Right. Well, then... I've sold the business.'

'What?'

'That's right. The whole lot. It's why Caroline upped and left me. Thought she'd be jetting round all of the hotels and acting the Empress.'

That wasn't breaking news. She'd certainly passed on quite a few 'style choices' to Noah she had thought his father should make in the exclusive hotel he owned in Sydney. All of them in direct contrast to the elegant, discreet interior decor his mother had chosen. Caroline had been overruled.

His father gave his head a rub. 'That's a lot of spare dosh I've got floating around, and I'd like to see it put to good use.'

Noah went on the defensive. 'I'm not moving back to Sydney.'

'And I'm not asking you to.'

Both he and Rebecca back, surprised. 'What *are* you asking?' they said as one. Then turned to each other and laughed. 'Snap!'

'Oh, for heaven's sake…' Noah's father waved his hands. 'You two lovebirds…' His expression softened.

'What, Dad?'

'You remind me of me and your mother back in the day.'

Now, this was another surprise.

His dad leant back in his chair, and after a moment tugging at an invisible thread he said, 'I know I was a horrible husband. Unfaithful. Unkind. I took out all my insecurities on your mother when she was my number one champion. She gave me you two kids.' He winced at his turn of phrase. 'I should've been a much better father. I'll never be able to make up for the father I was, but I plan to start becoming the one I should have been.'

'Right…' Noah was wary. 'And what does that involve?'

'I'd like to invest in the clinic here. Donate, really. And also start a school. One the girls can go to for a Class-A education.'

'There are already schools here, Dad.'

'Yeah, but not ones that offer scholarships to the type of kiddies you're treating here.'

Rebecca jumped in. 'You want to subsidise medical treatment and education for the poor?'

'That's right.' Noah's dad pointed at Rebecca while nodding at Noah. 'She's got the idea. Bright one, this little chicken. You'd better tell me she's a keeper.'

Though he was still reeling from his father's about-face—from global entrepreneur to local philanthropist—Noah had enough wherewithal to know what his priority was. 'I'm going to do everything in my power to keep her by my side.'

Rebecca grinned and gave him a playful elbow in the ribs. 'I think we've got a few particulars to iron out first.'

'Like?'

'Like you receiving my nan's stamp of approval, for one.'

He grinned, looking forward to the moment when the woman who'd raised the love of his life arrived. 'I'll be buffing all my shoes in the morning.' He pretended to write it down. 'Anything else she'll want to see shipshape?'

'Definitely. But I don't want to scare you off.' She made a scary face.

He could tell from her cheeky smile that she was joking…but also not joking. She wanted to be taken seriously. To be treated as a partner, not as the person who put in all the graft to lay the foundations for a relationship only to discover she'd built something her other half had never wanted to stand on.

'Don't you worry. It'll take an army of nay-sayers to frighten me off. And even then…' He made a couple of martial arts moves, to her obvious amusement.

Rebecca grinned, holding up her phone. 'You'd better get yourself battle-ready, because she's arriving here in a week.'

'Hold still, Nan. I just need to straighten these flowers in your hair.' Rebecca pinned the tropical flowers in place, their scent mingling organically with her grandmother's familiar perfume as she did. It was still so hard to believe her nan had flown all the way out here with Nathan and announce they were also getting married. When she finished, they both stepped back, hand in hand, to look at one another.

'You look beautiful,' her nan pronounced.

'Well, so do you. And, as the bride to be, you're the one who matters the most.'

Noah knocked on the door, letting out a low whistle of approval. 'Nathan is one lucky man!'

Nanny Bea cackled, waving away Noah's approval. 'You're just saying that to get on my good side, young man.' She fixed him with her best steely gaze. 'You know, the minister said he's happy to do a double wedding.'

Rebecca and Noah looked at one another's matching expressions of horror and then, after Nanny Bea had excused herself to the spare room to finish her make-up, realised they were actually letting the idea sink in and marinate.

'You are dressed very beautifully,' Noah said with an appreciative wink. 'Best-looking bridesmaid I've ever seen.'

'And your suit's very nice. Linen suits you.' Rebecca wasn't even looking at the suit. She was staring directly into Noah's eyes, trying to see if he was feeling what she was. Fear and excitement. Hope and possibility. 'Not that I've imagined it much…' she teased. 'For some reason I pictured you in scrubs when— I mean if we were ever to marry.'

'I'm happy to change,' Noah volunteered, half turning towards the stairs. 'I'm sure I can find a bow tie somewhere. Dad's probably brought one.'

They both grinned at the image.

'Would your father approve?'

'Of the bow tie?' Noah asked. 'Probably not. Of you?' he added more seriously. 'From the moment he saw you. Just like me.'

'And there's the girls to tell. Do you think they'll be happy?'

Noah tipped his head back and forth, nodding, and said, 'Actually, they brought me this this morning…just in case.' He dipped into his pocket and pulled out a seashell that had been worn through by the sea so that it was shaped like a ring.

Rebecca's hands flew to cover her mouth. 'It's beautiful.'

'Born from the sea. Just as I first saw you. My very own Amphitrite.'

A goddess of the sea. It wasn't how she'd ever once imagined herself. Then again, six months ago she never would have believed she would have left her future to a coin-toss and ended up in love with her soul mate in Bali.

'What if the universe delivers bad things?'

'The universe brings good and bad all the time,' Noah reminded her as he closed the space between them and took her hands in his. 'We never would have met if my sister hadn't died. Or if your ex hadn't left you. We met each other when neither of us was at our best, and yet somehow we knew we could be better. Together.'

It was true. She closed her eyes and tried to imagine what her world would be like if things had gone according to her spreadsheet. To her astonishment, nothing appeared. When she opened her eyes, her heart skipped a beat. He was still there, holding her hands, offering himself as a pillar to lean on when she wavered.

She put on a mock-officious voice. 'Nanny Bea will need new witnesses for her marriage.'

Noah gave her a hard, serious look. 'Let's witness this wedding for her. Let her bask in the sunlight today with Nathan. Then, later,' he nuzzled into the nook between her ear and her collarbone and gave her a kiss, 'We'll marry with the pair of them as our witnesses.' He pulled back and looked at her. 'I want to ask you to marry me properly.'

Rebecca held up the shell ring then signalled to Noah to slip it onto her finger. 'Shall we call this a promise ring?'

'A promise of a lifetime together? Absolutely.' He slid the ring on her finger and as it shifted into place Rebecca felt something shift inside her heart. She felt lighter and more secure all at the same time. She felt whole.

A flight of butterflies lifted and fluttered round her tummy as she lost herself in Noah's eyes. They glittered with a happiness she hadn't seen in them before. Perhaps it was something deeper. Something approaching the contentment, the peace they both sought. Perhaps this was what her serenity coach had been guiding her towards all along: harmony. Because that was what she felt when she was with Noah Cameron.

Through the window she could see the minister taking his place and the musicians begin to warm up their instruments for the bridal march her nan had insisted on them playing.

'Shall we go watch two little lovebirds tie the knot?' she asked.

'I couldn't think of anything I'd rather do,' Noah dropped a kiss on her lips that promised so much more. A lifetime of love, happiness and mutual respect.

'C'mon.' She tugged his hands. 'Let's get the rest of our lives started.'

EPILOGUE

REBECCA LOOKED AROUND the newly refurbished
children's ward at The Island Clinic. The walls
had been painted in beautiful murals that made it
look as if it was in the heart of the Sacred Monkey Sanctuary. Large, wonderfully equipped
aquariums were built right into the walls, sky-
lights glowed with the filtered light coming
through the palm trees, and in the centre of the
waiting area was a wishing well.

Most of the furniture was for children—small
tables and chairs for arts and crafts, bean bags
and all sorts—but there were discreet nooks
where parents could tuck themselves away from
it all if they needed some time to regroup before
putting on a smile for their child.

While it could not be more perfect—beautifully designed and kitted out precisely for the
needs of children unfortunate enough to need to
stay in hospital—it was strange seeing it from
her current perspective: wearing a hospital gown

and being pushed round in a wheelchair. Then again, it was also completely unfamiliar to be holding her own child in her arms.

She looked down at the tiny little baby in her arms, then traced her finger along her infant's cheek. 'What do you think, love? Has your granddad done your namesake proud?'

'I'll say he has.' Noah pulled a chair over so that he was sitting beside them. He gently put his arm round Rebecca's shoulder and held out one of his fingers so that Indah, their two-day-old little girl, could clasp it in her tiny hand.

Ruby, who had been pushing Rebecca's wheelchair, came round to stand in front of the pair of them and asked if she and Isla could take the baby over to one of the aquariums.

'Of course, love. Here you go.'

Ruby smiled up at her grandfather, who had become a bit of a permanent fixture around the clinic. Even though he'd bought a very ritzy house a few miles away, 'to give them space', more often than not he was here at the clinic, now an impressive hospital, 'popping in'. He said it was to make sure things were being done to his specs, but Rebecca knew better. He was loving being part of a happy, growing family. He'd even built a bungalow in his garden for Nanny Bea and Nathan to stay in during their visits.

'Will wonders never cease?' Noah nodded towards his father, who was being taught how to skip by Isla as Ruby carefully carried the baby over to one of the huge aquariums.

Rebecca smiled at her husband. 'You know what? I don't think they do cease. It seems like the more we open our eyes to the good things in life, the more they just keep on appearing.'

Noah swept a couple of locks of hair away from her forehead. 'You had me worried the other day.'

She tipped her forehead to his. 'I know...' Her labour had been long and difficult, and in the end she'd had to have a Caesarean section in the brand-new maternity ward. 'I had me worried too. But...' She popped a kiss on Noah's nose. 'It was kind of amazing that we had the first baby on the new ward, wasn't it?'

'It wasn't just amazing, my love,' Noah said decisively. 'It was destiny.' He brushed her cheek with his lips and whispered, 'I hope you know how much I love you.'

'I do,' she whispered back. 'I do, I do, I do, I do, I *do*.'

* * * * *